P9-CQJ-204

TRACKERS

PATRICK CARMAN

TRACKERS

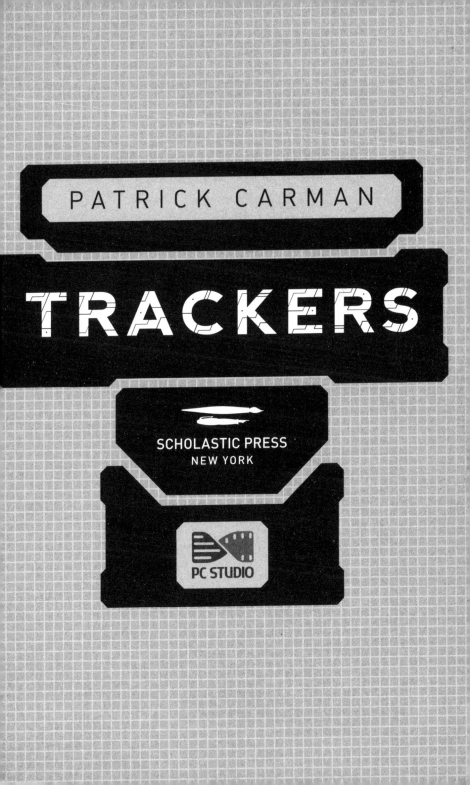

Library of Congress Cataloging-in-Publication Data
Available

ISBN 978-0-545-16500-6

10 9 8 7 6 5 4 3 2 1 10 11 12 13 14

Printed in the U.S.A. 23
First edition, May 2010

The text was set in Adobe Garamond Pro.
Book design by Christopher Stengel

*For George Hall,
who watched over me when
I needed it most*

LOCATION: Classified. Web-enabled mobile computer not present. Present, provided by subject: communication devices, surveillance videos, journals, loose paper documents, photographs, cameras, diagrams, audio recordings — all in view. Data extremely sensitive in nature.

SECURITY CLEARANCE: RED

SUBJECT: Adam Henderson. Records indicate elevated IQ and potentially dangerous personality traits.

Digital taping initiated at 16:35 Pacific Standard Time, Tuesday, August 12.

Subject Adam Henderson would not respond to questioning during first seven minutes.

Subject spoke at 16:42.

A. HENDERSON: Is this being recorded?

Subject was informed of multiple video cameras and audio recording devices in use.

A. HENDERSON: Good. I only want to do this once.

My colleagues left the room, entered surveillance area behind two-way mirror.

We are all watching him.

He has begun.

How far back can you go, Adam?

What do you mean?

I think you know what I mean. Start at the beginning.

The very beginning?

Yes. I need to know everything.

There's no way for you to know everything. We'd be in here for a month.

What I mean is — don't hold anything back. If you think it's relevant, I want to know about it.

Like I have a choice.

Yes, you do. The ball is in your court. You can play this however you like. Just remember, it's not only your future on the line here. This is about a lot more people than you, Adam Henderson.

Subject stared coldly at the two-way mirror, appeared to be weighing his options one last time. He has all the answers stored in his mind, waiting to be downloaded. Everything we need is in there, if only I can get him moving in the right direction.

It began with a guy who went camping all by himself in the 1960s and got lost. I mean, like, *really* lost.

Adam, I don't think we need to go back fifty years. That's not what I meant.

You want the whole story or don't you?

I want the whole story.

Then stop interrupting me.

It was a huge forest, bigger than five counties, full of bears and cougars and rattlers. The forest service sent in this old tracker — a big-bearded, long-haired, cowboy hat–wearing mountain man, the last of his kind. *They don't make 'em like that anymore* — that's what everybody said about this tracker dude. He didn't work for the government or the police or anything like that. He lived deep in the woods and knew its secrets. A real tracker knows his terrain inside and out.

It took him three days of walking in the wild all alone in the cold and the rain to find what he was looking for: a man sitting with his back against a tree, miles from anything resembling a trail, holding nothing but an empty water bottle in one hand and a Buck knife in the other. The tracker looked down and said, and I quote, "Get up off your sorry butt. We got some walking to do."

Believe it or not this guy — the tracker in the story — he wasn't just any mountain man, he was my grandfather. I realize this is hard to believe, given the way I live, but it's the plain truth, and it's important.

I never met Old Henderson, which is what my dad calls my grandfather when he tells me these stories, because Old Henderson met up with a grizzly one day and never came back. My dad was just a kid, so, as you might imagine, this took the shine off the outdoors. He hated the woods after that, moved to Seattle the first chance he got, and never looked back.

Why are you telling me these things, Adam?

Because my urban existence doesn't change a thing about where I came from. My grandfather was a legendary tracker, in a mud-under-his-fingernails sort of way. And more than that, he had a knack for landing himself in the most dangerous situations. You know how family traits have a way of skipping a generation, then returning with a vengeance? I may not be much for snakes and grizzlies, or carrying a heavy backpack, but the tracking part is in my blood. Give me a room full of computers and cell phones and I'll find anyone you want, sometimes the most dangerous people on earth. Because here's the thing about the digital age: Everyone leaves a trail.

Some of them shouldn't be followed.

16:52

So you considered yourself a tracker?

Yes. All of us were trackers. We found things. It's what we did.

By hacking into computers —

No. Look, if you're going to do that, we can just stop right now. Hacking is when you break into places in order to mess them up. Believe me, I've seen plenty of hacking, and that's not what we were into. We did the opposite. We were trying to keep people safe, not put them in danger.

Only that didn't work, did it?

We never meant to hurt anybody. Or ourselves.

You had no idea the level of danger you were in?

I thought you wanted to start at the beginning. I thought you wanted to hear *everything.*

I do. Tell me about your father, then. After he left the wilderness and brought you into the world of computers.

By the time I was old enough to walk, my dad had started Henderson's Chip Shop in Seattle, which had the distinction of being the best computer repair store on the planet. When I was five he put me to work taking apart hard drives, and by the time

I was eight I was fixing pretty much anything he dropped in front of me.

For a kid, Henderson's Chip Shop was like a giant Lego factory, where all the parts and pieces were circuit boards, monitors, cords, buttons, and drives. As far as I was concerned, it was heaven on earth.

On my ninth birthday my dad walked me through the clutter of piled-up computers, monitors, and printers until we were at the very back of the store, where customers were never allowed. For as long as I could remember there had been floor-to-ceiling shelves of parts and boxes back there, but on this day, a section of the shelves had been removed. I was surprised to see that something more than just a wall had been hidden behind the shelves for all those years.

"Where does it lead?" I asked, staring at the scuffed white door that had been revealed.

My dad had his big hands on my shoulders, standing behind me.

"Happy birthday, Dr. Destructo," he said. It was an inside joke between the two of us, because I liked using a hammer whenever possible. It was not uncommon in those days to find me wailing away on a hard drive, trying to get a very small part to jog loose from its casing.

My dad had stenciled *The Vault* onto the door in black paint. When I opened it, I nearly fell over. There were outlets. There was a bench. There was a light. My hammer was in there.

My dad knelt down next to me and we both stared inside.

"Consider it your laboratory," he said, nodding toward the door. "Anything that gets left behind, you can have." The Vault was small and stuffy, like a closet, but it was mine. I turned around and hugged my dad as if he'd just given me a dirt bike, twelve thousand candy bars, and another dirt bike.

In the months that followed I realized that Henderson's Chip Shop was, among other things, a dumping ground. It was common for people to bring in a relic for repair without any intention of ever picking it up again. You could see it in their eyes, hauling in a five-year-old computer box and setting it heavily on the counter like a ball and chain they were about to unhitch from their leg. A week would go by, maybe two, and the writing was on the wall.

The Vault would devour it.

My little corner of the universe may not sound like much, but it was everything I could have hoped for and more. I'd been given my own private space to tinker. I could expect an endless supply of technological junk to pass across my workbench. I would be like Steve Jobs inventing the Apple computer or Bill Gates cobbling together the first operating system. The Vault was mine, and I would fill it with my inventions and my ideas. It was basically love at first sight.

And this was when you were nine?

Yes.

You were doing all of these things?

Yeah. I know my idea of a good time was not entirely normal for a nine-year-old. It's just what I did.

You were a prodigy?

I hate that word. But yeah, I guess so. Only my instrument wasn't a piano or languages or a chessboard, it was technology. No one had to tell me how to decipher code or connect the right wires; I just knew. It was like a musical language I was born with. My mom used to call me Mozart with a mouse, which I think is pretty accurate.

My parents were prone to extremely quiet and solitary behavior — dad with his hardware, mom with her endless, private writing — so it was normal for us to become engrossed in our own small worlds, contentedly hammering away at whatever we were working on.

By the time I hit fifth grade the Vault had turned me into a hi-tech hermit. I spent my time by myself, but I was also wired to hundreds, if not thousands, of other people. The wall above the workbench was my masterpiece, covered in monitors, keyboards, and computers strung together. I had enough processing power and bandwidth to run the most devastatingly complex software, a lot of which I created myself. I ran dozens of surveillance cameras all over the city just for fun, using hardware I developed myself, encased in small, nondescript housings of metal that made you think they belonged on those telephone poles. I ran online stores, selling battle-axes to gamers and digital clothing for avatars. I made piles of virtual money and used it to buy all the newest gadgets, laptops, phones, and cameras. I ripped apart everything I bought, and I was never afraid of using the same hammer I'd always used when nothing else would do the trick.

I was especially good at tracking. I'd choose a big company online and find out everything I could about them. I'd give myself time limits. If I found a really bad breach in security, I'd anonymously let the company know. You know the word *firewall*? Well, it's way too accurate. Because the thing about a wall of fire? You can walk through it if you have the right gear. I would find the more penetrable parts and then help people make them less penetrable.

Fourth and fifth grades were incredibly productive in the Vault. I was making real progress toward my goal of total world domination. I was earning enough virtual dough to buy stuff no ten-year-old should be allowed to play with. I had contacts all over the world, asking me to test their codes and begging me to buy gadgets they'd somehow gotten their hands on through means I knew better than to ask about. I got smartphones with features that wouldn't be on the market for years. And what did I do with them? I tore them open, taking out the best parts. There were Brontobyte drives, which held more stuff than even I thought was possible — think of a number with twenty-seven zeros behind it; you could store that many YouTube videos on a Brontobyte drive. I invented the WaffleIron, a Wi-Fi sucking monster that gave me more bandwidth than the Pentagon. I had turned the Vault into a world-class hi-tech laboratory, my own fortress.

Then sixth grade rolled up and hit me like a bus.

Why was sixth grade different?

Grade school was such a cake assignment, not so much because the work was beyond easy, but because the social scene was super basic. No one really bugged me. I went. I did my time. I played wall ball like I was supposed to. After school I went back to the Vault and ripped open a cell phone or two. Life was good.

Middle school was just as easy, academically speaking, but the social part was something I wasn't prepared for. There were skateboarders, BMXers, athletes, thespians, dancers, singers, student council members, and a dozen other cliques, none of which I took the slightest interest in. The Vault had robbed me of any desire to fit in and make friends. But watching all these kids in their groups of three or five or ten, I started to feel something I hadn't felt before. Something about walking the halls, day after day, not talking to anyone — I guess it changed me.

For the first time in my life, I was lonely.

Even with all of the contact you had with people in the virtual world?

Yes. It's not the same. Believe me, my first reaction was to spend even more time in the Vault, surfing the Net until all hours, disconnected from the real world. I was making some of my best stuff, focused as I was, and it was all screaming *Hey! Adam! Go find some real friends!* I say this because the things I was making were completely useless for a hermit. It was as if my mind had secretly played a trick on me, making me invent things that would force me out of my solitude.

And that's when you met the other Trackers.

Finn first.

At school?

No. The first time I met Finn was at the bus stop downtown when I should have been in second-period math. He blasted by on his skateboard, skidded to a stop, and came back.

"Hey, I know you," he said.

I didn't say anything, gripping the straps on my backpack until my knuckles turned white. What I knew about Finn was that he was friendly with almost everyone and skipped school a lot. I didn't want anything to do with him as he kicked his board up into his hand.

He said something like, "I mean, I don't *know* you, but I've seen you. Over at Davis, right?"

I glanced down the street, searching for the city bus, and wished I hadn't slipped out of school a half hour before. Skipping? What was I, crazy? At the time it was a fairly new concept for me.

"Not too chatty, huh? I can respect that," Finn said. He sat down next to me on the bus stop bench and spun the front wheels on his board. "Where you goin'?"

"Home," I said, surprised by my own voice. It didn't sound too friendly.

"That's cool," he said. "Home's good. Maybe you'll get some cookies and a glass of milk."

"Not likely," I told him. I would have to sneak back in and hide in the Vault, hoping my parents were too busy to notice.

Finn nodded, dropped his board in front of me, and proceeded to practice kick flips over and over again. On the sixth try the board flipped out from under him and flew down the sidewalk. Finn landed hip first on the pavement with a crack and didn't move.

"You okay?" I asked.

Finn just lay there, not moving, like he was dead. I would come to learn that this was his way of overcoming pain and humiliation on four wheels, but at the time, I seriously considered calling 911. After about ten seconds Finn rolled over slowly and sat up, pulling a cell phone out of his back pocket.

"I knew I shouldn't have put that there."

The screen on the phone looked like I'd taken my hammer to it, and the lonely kid inside me saw the opportunity I'd been searching for. I told him I'd trade phones, if he was interested.

I pulled my backpack off and unzipped it, yanking out one of my inventions. It was a super early model, nothing close to what I'm making now, and it didn't look anything like a modern cell phone.

Finn laughed as he stood up and jogged over to retrieve his board. When he rolled back he was shaking his head.

"Fred Flintstone give you that thing?" he asked.

I stared at the brick-sized phone I was holding, with its foot-long antenna sticking out the top. It was true the thing was enormous and clunky, but it had its advantages.

"This is way better than the phone you've got," I told him. "There's no cell phone bill."

Finn ripped the monstrous device out of my hand and inspected the old-school keyboard and tiny screen.

"No bill?" he asked.

"No bill," I told him. "I promise. And it's got a built-in video camera. And a GPS. And a laser pointer, in case you need to do a presentation. Oh, and it's waterproof."

And illegal.

No, it was perfectly legal. I was telling the truth about never getting a cell phone bill, because I had over three million minutes piled up in reserve, traded for virtual cash online.

So you became partners.

No. We became friends.

Does that make you regret what happened?

We knew what we were doing. We all knew what we were doing.

But then?

But then, I guess, it all spun out of control.

17:14

So how did you meet the other Trackers?

Emily and Lewis were friends of Finn's. I became a part of their group. Pretty simple, really.

Tell me more about them. Emily and Lewis. Before everything happened. Before things spun out of control.

I don't know. They're just Emily and Lewis.

But when you first met them, what did you think?

So let me get this straight — you don't want to hear the thrilling adventures of my grizzly-mauled grandfather, but you're all interested in the lives of my friends three years ago? You're a real piece of work.

Don't push your luck, Adam. I'm giving you a shot here. You want a chance at a normal life? You want that for your friends? Then you better get serious about this investigation.

Okay, okay — you got my attention. Take it easy. You want Lewis and Emily at twelve, you got it.

Proceed.

When I met Lewis for the first time, I thought he was going to throw up on my shoes. He was *that* nervous to meet me. Lewis was a typical young tech geek: not comfortable around new people, obsessed with video games, uneasy about making big decisions that could lead to an awkward situation. I'd never met a person who was so methodical about making a decision. Something as simple as "Let's go get a pizza" would lead to a series of questions about who might be there, how much it would cost, and what the overall risks were. This would prove helpful later on, but mostly, it drove us all crazy in the early days.

There was another reason Lewis was so nervous to meet me. He knew who I was, even if Finn didn't. The thing you have to realize is that Finn is not a prototypical computer nerd like me and Lewis. In our group, Finn is actually the oddball. Back then, if he had been into all the stuff me and Lewis were into, Finn would have thought differently about me. I had a certain, I don't know, reputation, I guess, in the online world based in Seattle. I was, you know . . .

A legend.

Whatever. The point is Lewis knew about some of what I'd done. I'd solved some really tough contest equations, programmed security scripts Microsoft was using, you know, stuff like that. I'll never forget shaking Lewis's hand in front of the school. Clammy and limp, like a dead fish. He said "hey," jumped on his bike, and tore off down the street. We never even made eye contact. For the record, he's gotten a lot better. For sure. He's amazing, actually.

And Emily?

First time I met her she almost beat me up for scaring Lewis. I'm like, "All I did was shake the guy's hand!" But she was very protective of him, kind of like a big sister I guess. She wasn't interested in the whole boy-crazy scene back then, always wore a baseball cap. And that's not to say she couldn't have had plenty of dates. I mean, you've seen her — she's far from ugly.

The thing is, Emily can be sort of pushy. When Lewis took off that day she looked at me and said, "You gave Finn a phone that never gets a bill. Got any more?" That was Emily, down to business from the word *go*.

And when did they first find out about you?

What do you mean?

When did you show them all the things you could do? For example, when did you first show them the Vault?

What you really mean is, how did we make the leap from friends to Trackers? I get it.

Okay, fine. How did you become Trackers?

It started with Finn. He's not a programmer. He's not even into computers. But Finn seemed to know everything about everyone, including the dirt. So he comes to us one day, like a week after I joined the group, and he says, "Someone's taking skateboards."

I remember Emily jumping right in, shaking her head as if she knew where this was going. "No way, uh-uh, Finn, we're not getting involved. Remember what happened last time?"

"What happened last time?" I asked. I hadn't been around them long enough to know that Finn had a habit of dragging Emily and Lewis into all sorts of things they'd otherwise avoid.

"Go ahead, tell him," Emily said, staring at Finn. But then

she kept going before Finn could "misrepresent the facts" and I sat next to Lewis listening to her go on and on about a missing video game from Finn's locker. It didn't end well, because Finn had convinced Lewis to break open a half dozen other lockers, sure he'd find the missing game — picking locks being one of Lewis's hidden skills. They both got suspended for two days, during which Finn played the missing video game endlessly. Turns out it was under his bed the whole time.

I remember the rest of the argument like it was yesterday, maybe because it has played out in other situations so many times since.

Emily said, "You can't go dragging us into your crazy schemes all the time."

Finn shot back, "Lewis can speak for himself, right, Lewis?"

Lewis looked at me with an expression that said *you see what I have to deal with?* I felt cornered, like I was the deciding vote in something I didn't fully comprehend. All I could offer Lewis was a lame shrug of my shoulders.

It might have been Lewis trying to impress me, might have been he just couldn't tell Finn no. Either way, we were on our first stakeout a few hours later.

What do four twelve-year-olds do on a stakeout?

Probably a lot more than you might imagine. We installed wireless cameras — hard to get in those days — at the outdoor skate park in question, then I took the group to the Vault for the first time. I'd never let anyone in there before but my dad and my mom, so it was a big deal for me. I fired up the wall of monitors as Finn picked up gadgets and parts that weren't nailed down and asked, over and over again, "What's this thing do?"

Lewis and Emily stood in the small space, staring at the wall of electronics with expressions of awe and reverence. They got it. They instantly knew how special the Vault was.

"Is that what I think it is?" Lewis asked me as the monitors blazed with fuzzy black-and-white images. We were watching the skate park across town from four different angles. I handed Lewis and Emily each a swivel joystick and let them change the directions of the views while they zoomed in and out.

"Adam, you're twelve," Emily reminded me. "How did you do all this? You must have had help."

But I hadn't had any help at all, and they'd seen only a fraction of what I'd done at that point. This was three years ago, and I can tell you one thing: The stuff we were doing back then was child's play compared to the things we did this summer.

Anyway, a few days later we caught a teenager on tape, lifting a skateboard while the owner was in the concrete block bathroom. We staked out the park and took color photos of the thief when he returned the next day. Then we sent the tape and the pictures, anonymously, to the city police department with a note that read: *Tall teenager, long hair, baseball cap, stealing boards. Hope you catch him.*

Sounds like they brought you out of your shell.

If it weren't for them I'm positive I would have made my parents homeschool me. Finn, Emily, Lewis — they were the ones who rescued me. They got me through middle school.

And this is how you repay them.

Thanks. That makes me feel a lot better.

I think that's enough backstory to satisfy my curiosity. You're rolling now. It's time you jumped to the present. Tell me what happened this summer.

You know I have a highly developed memory, right?

I figured that out, yes.

I remember what they said. I remember it all. It's just how my brain works. You're going to think I'm crazy, but it's like I have a video recorder in my head and I can rewind it. I've never used it this way before, but I want to tell you what happened exactly as it occurred. It's the only way you're going to know the whole truth.

Adam, I don't care how you tell me. Just tell me.

Understood.

17:22

With eighth grade behind us and summer staring us in the face, I knew from experience that Finn was never going to master the skill of being on time, *especially* if it was important. I was sitting in the Vault, ripping the wire guts out of a Wii, when Emily piped in.

"Why am I not surprised?" she asked.

It wasn't in Emily's personality to let a guy like Finn off the hook too easily. She had no patience for this kind of thing.

"I can hear you grinding out there!" she said anxiously, unable to let it rest. "It's kind of obvious you're not actually riding *toward* us."

"Oh, you heard that." Finn laughed, taking it all in stride like he always did. It took a lot to rattle Finn. "No worries, I'll be there in two shakes."

I remember this: Emily asked, "What is 'two shakes'? What does that even mean?" I remember her staring down at me with a puzzled look on her face. There were six monitors in the Vault, one of which showed Emily's face. She was staring into her phone from a remote location near the waterfront.

"It means he'll be there when he gets done skating," I offered, tossing the Wii casing into a pile on the floor.

"So true!" yelled Finn.

He was obviously in the middle of some crazy move I wouldn't dare try without a football helmet on my head and ten pillows duct taped to my body. I admired his perfect mix of laid-back chill and out-of-control skating skills.

The Green Lantern was housed in an early 1900s waterfront warehouse with boarded-up windows and padlocked entrance.

They allowed only the best skaters in there, and I'd rarely been inside. It was very exclusive.

"Adam, you there?" asked Finn. I gazed at the wall of monitors in the Vault and found Finn staring into his camera. He was constantly putting his face too close to the lens so his nose looked huge and out of proportion.

"Dude, back up, you're scaring me," I told him.

Finn ignored me and kept right on talking. I could tell he'd left the Green Lantern and started riding toward Emily.

"I might have busted another Belinski," he said. "Can I get a new one for the test?"

Belinski?

The Belinski was an all-purpose camera Finn could mount on the front of his skateboard. It was the easiest device to make, and I usually had three or four backups in the Vault. Still, I couldn't help giving Finn a bad time.

"I just gave you a new one yesterday! Are you kidding me?"

As always, Finn tried to get out of the blame. "Not my fault, truly," he said. "I got chased by a dog and things got crazy. The camera still works, but the lens is busted."

"Was it a poodle or a Chihuahua?" Emily asked.

"Lewis, tell him," Finn shouted, hopping a curb as his face jumped wildly across the monitor. "You were there. Big dog, right?"

Lewis stared into his camera from where he sat on his BMX.

"Are we doing the test, or has this thing been rescheduled?" he asked. "I could imagine eating a Hot Pocket and wasting a few Orcs."

Lewis was a gamer, like me, and we were on a rampage through Exodar, taking swipes at Magnataurs in *World of Warcraft*.

"We're *doing* the test," said Emily, staring straight at me through her own mobile camera. "Which means you need to get out of the Vault and on your scooter."

What kind of test?

I had been laser-focused on surveillance for a couple of years, sure that the stuff I was developing would be huge with security firms and government agencies. What the Trackers didn't always understand was that field tests were critical to developing new software and hardware. Everything was carefully planned to give me important data I would go through later. For the gang it was a cool game they'd come to love, but for me, field tests were serious business. I knew that tracking was equal parts gear and skill.

So you joined them?

I turned off my camera and heard Emily asking for a mobile visual, but I wasn't ready to leave the Vault just yet. I needed a few minutes to think. Six street view cameras with motion detection were in place. Emily had the Trinity camera, the most sensitive of the bunch with frame-by-frame slow-motion capture I'd developed myself. That was an expensive unit, and hard to fix if it went down. Lewis was trained and ready on the Deckard, a high-definition masterpiece with a software zoom that rivaled the most advanced lenses anywhere. I had two spare Belinskis in my bag for Finn, and Emily had another in her backpack if things got out of hand. The Belinski was a solid, basic unit that was also easily broken, especially when it was in Finn's hands.

I shut down the Vault and locked the door, throwing on my backpack as I headed for the front door of Henderson's Chip Shop. My dad was head down over a hard drive and barely nodded as I passed by his workbench.

He had no idea what you were doing?

None. He's completely innocent. He had nothing to do with any of it.

So you never thought of the trouble you might get him into?

I'm telling you — it had nothing to do with him. Like that day, he was completely oblivious as I fired up the Roadrunner, my electric-powered scooter, and blasted down the sidewalk toward the waterfront.

Five minutes of zipping down sidewalks and back alleys landed me in an empty parking lot with the rest of the Trackers, where I went through every detail of our plan one last time. And ten minutes after that? The field test, which turned out to be a disaster, was over.

A disaster?

Look — I can show you. I've kept everything perfectly organized in a secret place. I've never let anyone in there but Emily, Finn, and Lewis, but if you're going to understand everything that happened to us, I'm going to have to give you access. It makes me nervous letting an outsider in, but I don't think there's any other way. I've set it up so you'll see only what I want you to see, when I want you to see it. If there's one thing I can't stand, it's someone getting their hands on information they're not ready for. Information is always misinterpreted out of context. And don't bother trying to hack the system — it's impossible. I'll reveal what I want, when I want. It's the only way everything will make sense.

Okay. We're following your lead, Adam.

I need a computer.

We'll get you one.

Interview notation:
To maintain the illusion it's just him and me, I leave the room and return with a laptop. Watching Adam size it up gives me insight into the way he works — he figures out the machine quickly, the way we try to figure out people. He gets the feel of it immediately. He knows how to make it do what he wants it to do. He sees hidden things.

Nice try on the tracing software. I hope you don't mind, but I've disabled it. Did you know I wrote some of the underlying code?

No, I didn't know that. You've got your fingers in a lot of places it seems.

You don't know the half of it.

I have a funny feeling I don't know a *tenth* of it. What are you going to show me?

The evidence is stored in parts on many different servers. When I enter the right password the code connects across a network, like a puzzle, and creates something you can find. I've also activated a portion of my RMS system for you. The RMS is a mapping tool I developed that will show you exactly where Henderson's Chip Shop is. As I tell you more, the RMS will reveal additional locations so you'll know precisely where everything happened. And if you want to see what the Trinity, Deckard, and Belinski mobile units are all about, I've uploaded detailed widgets on those, too.

Check it out. This is how the Trackers roll.

Interview notation:
This interface is still live. If you enter the password, you will see what I saw during this interview. A transcript appears in Appendix A, page 154.

www.trackersinterface.com

PASSWORD

STROGNOFE993

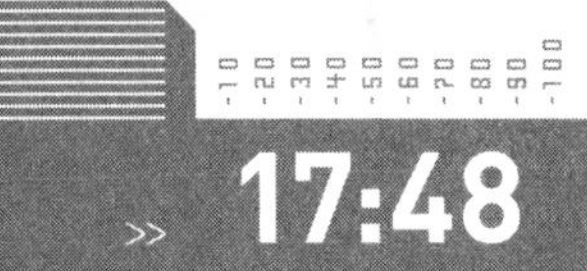

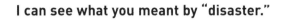

I can see what you meant by "disaster."

Giving expensive equipment to teenagers has its risks, but come on, *three* broken cameras? It was a new record, or a new low, depending on how I looked at it. I tallied up the damage, totally amazed at the devastation:

- Finn smashes a Belinski swinging his skateboard into a timing marker.
- Lewis drops the Deckard camera into the bay.
- And Emily, not to be outdone, attaches the Trinity to a remote-control hot rod and sends it into a flaming death spiral.

It all happened so fast. I still watch that video and can't believe the destruction of so much precious hardware in such a small span of time.

But you persisted?

Of course. You can't just give up. It was a training mission.

No matter what the cost?

You keep hinting at the idea that we knew more than we did. I'm telling you, we had no idea what was about to happen.

How did the others react to the failure of your "test"?

Finn said, "Hey, at least mine was cheap."

We would always debrief at the Grind House, our favorite café hangout, which is right down the street from Henderson's.

"None of them are cheap," I corrected. "Some are just less outrageously expensive."

But you could afford it, couldn't you? We've discovered records —

Yeah, I could afford it. I had more virtual cash from my online operations than I could reasonably trade for parts and services. Still, these pricey gadgets were hard to make, so I wanted to make Finn, Emily, and Lewis feel at least a *little* guilty. That's what friends do.

"I'm sorry, Adam, really I am," Emily confessed. She'd pulled a Mariners baseball cap low over her eyes, something she did whenever she was feeling low. "I don't know what got into me. I guess I really didn't want us to fail this time."

It wasn't like Emily to put Trinity in harm's way. She loved that device like it was a pet kitten.

"The Trinity is crazy expensive, huh?" Lewis responded. He was a penny-pincher and hated to spend money on anything he didn't have to. You'd think the guy had lived through the Depression. It was a tricky personality trait at a place like the Grind House, because the owner had a strange habit of randomly changing the prices on things from one day to the next.

"Actually, your camera will be tougher to replace than Emily's will be," I told Lewis. I wasn't trying to hurt his feelings — it was the truth.

"I've got a dozen players waiting for upgrades," Lewis said. "I'll send some your way." He was referring to all the gamers online who wanted hit points and levels, things we could sell in virtual dollars. A gamer could pay for that kind of thing, and Lewis and I had inventory to spare.

I thanked Lewis, but explained to him that it wasn't the cost that was the problem — it was the Deckard lens, which had to ship from Germany. At that point, I only had two Trinity backups, a half dozen Belinskis, and a single Deckard. I warned Lewis he'd have to be extra careful with the last one.

Emily beamed, thrilled that she'd be back in business right away, but Lewis was mortified. He was nervous by nature and didn't like any added pressure, but the Deckard was his camera. He'd trained for it and knew how to really push its capabilities in the field. And there was no way I was giving a Deckard to Finn. We had to hope our next test would go more smoothly.

"Good deal on cookies today," said Finn, trying to cheer Lewis up. The poor guy was sweating just thinking about carrying the only Deckard our team had. "Only eighty-five cents. I paid a buck ten on Friday."

"No, thanks," said Lewis. Then he picked himself up and made a half-baked excuse about having to check in with his parents back home. Finn was itching to get back to the Green Lantern and blow off some steam on the half-pipe, so Emily and I rode to the Vault together, me on the Roadrunner and her on an ivy-green mountain bike she rode everywhere.

"Can I stay awhile and review the footage with you?" she asked when we pulled up to Henderson's a couple of blocks away.

What I really wanted to do was pull a hermit move for the next ten hours or so. I figured I'd order a lens from my contact in Berlin and pre-build the Deckard casing first, a great way to wind down after a field test. The rest of the parts were easy — Xbox controller, flash drive, a micro-board, my own software, some

WaffleIron Wi-Fi and I'd have another one prepped. When the lens showed up, I'd be ready to roll. After that I'd review all the data that had streamed into the Vault during the test until after midnight.

But Emily was persistent. When she wanted something, it was hard to say no and I didn't feel like arguing.

"Come on," I said. "You can review Finn's wreckage while I build Lewis a new camera."

A few hours later I was done with the casing and Emily had entered a bunch of data into a spreadsheet for me. She was efficient and focused, which was something I appreciated in the Vault. The room barely held two people with how small it was and all the parts stacked up everywhere. We took a dinner break around six and I gave her a replacement Trinity camera, which left me only one spare. Emily fired it up, testing out all the functions while we ate and dialing in her favorite settings. I told her to maybe think twice before mounting it to a hot rod next time.

Emily smiled and tried to dial up Finn, who was nowhere to be found. We hailed Lewis, who kept us company at the table on Trinity's small screen, then Emily went home and I went back to my work.

You were looking at the footage from the day?

Yeah. And that's when I found something that changed the field test from a disastrous failure into a totally unexpected challenge.

What did you find?

The thing about the Deckard that makes it so cool is its incredible zoom capability. It's partly because of the very expensive lens, but more than that, it's the software I developed that takes images and breaks them down into pixels. Once the Deckard has a lock on something, it can zoom to almost microscopic levels. But the most important thing my software does is that it makes the zooming possible in video form. I can basically take any frame in post and zoom at levels previously thought impossible.

Lewis has the same zooming software at home as I do in the Vault, and usually it's his job to review his own material. But the Deckard was at the bottom of the bay, so this time it was up to me, pulling data from the feed his camera had sent to the Vault drives.

I'm a steady-as-she-goes sort of person, but as I looked over the footage I realized something that sent a chill up the back of my neck even as I sat in the stuffy back room of Henderson's Chip Shop.

Someone was watching us.

While Lewis and Emily waited for Finn to get into position, the Deckard scanned the street in both directions. It moved across several buildings, then settled on the front of the warehouse, where it panned back and forth. I still-framed the entry door and began zooming. Ten times, twenty times, thirty times the original size. The video pixels blurred and sharpened with every click of my mouse, until I was staring at the top left corner of the doorjamb.

A white business card had been slipped into the casing

around the door, and when I clicked my mouse again, I could read the printed text. Small black letters and a symbol I recognized, both on a crisp white background.

THE GLYPHMASTER AWAITS YOU.

Did you know who the Glyphmaster was?

No.

Not then.

No. Not then.

But you had an idea of what the message meant?

Yes and no. I had mixed feelings about the message as I stared at it on the screen. It was cool that someone was trying to communicate with us. Maybe it was a software company, like Google or Microsoft, and they'd taken an interest in our activity. The weird part, the part that made me a little nervous, was that they knew more about me than I was comfortable with. Whoever put the card there had definitely left it specifically for me and me alone.

How could you be sure?

The symbol on the card was my symbol. I'd made it. And not only that, the symbol represented me, Adam Henderson.

Look — there's no way of saying this without sounding like a complete geek, so I won't beat around the bush: The first time I saw *The Lord of the Rings*, I became obsessed with creating my own language. I thought if Tolkien could create his own languages (and he could, trust me) then I could do it, too.

I gathered the twenty-five smartest online contacts I had, none of whom appeared to have demanding social lives, and together we created a visual language called the Glyph. I'd never met any of these people and knew them only by their online exploits and coded names.

There was only one young programmer I wouldn't allow into the Glyph program from the start, because he was known for breaking into all sorts of things, and I was completely against associating with known hackers. Shantorian was his handle, and I knew him only by his legendary status. His name came up all the time, because he came up through the programming ranks at the same time I did, but he was incredibly good at hiding. Even if I'd wanted him in the group, I probably wouldn't have been able to find him.

So you never looked for him?

No.

Go on.

Creating the Glyph took forever, like a year, partly because we kept arguing about what words would get included and which ones would get the ax. The Glyph had no alphabet, no letters of any kind, and as the inventor of the language, I was dead set on only a hundred symbols. Connecting words like *a*, *and*, and *the* shared Glyphs, which meant we had more words than symbols.

Things were pretty heated. It got to the point where we had to vote on every single selection before it could be added into the Glyph. Buying off votes was rampant, and we had a voting fraud fiasco that led to the blacklisting of five members. These guys were so bent on including the word *booger* in the final cut that they hacked into the voting section of the site and rigged the outcome.

After upgrading security and finishing the word list, we developed a symbol generator and had to have a whole new set of arguments about what best represented each word in the Glyph. Trust me, *booger* would have been easy compared to some of the words we had to turn into visuals. Try making the word *might* into a symbol and you'll understand what I mean. We argued endlessly, voted on everything, and basically drove each other insane.

When the Glyph was complete, each of the remaining members created a personal Glyph symbol, one that represented themselves. By that time there were only twelve of us, everyone else having quit or been expelled for various reasons. I took it as a bad sign that seven of the personal symbols were of a finger inside a nose. The booger prevailed in the end.

You're funny, Mr. Henderson. Were the other Trackers part of this?

No. This was my thing. And it didn't even matter, because a week after it was a wrap the project collapsed under the weight of its own lameness. What little fun was to be had was in the making, not the using, and the Glyph fell quickly into obscurity, like an ancient, forgotten language. Even I forgot about it — until I saw the image flashing on my screen from Lewis's camera.

Note: A list of a hundred of Adam Henderson's Glyphs has been included here in Appendix B, page 162. Fifty remain unidentified by suspect.

So what did you do next? After you saw the card in the video.

I guzzled a monster hit off my Mountain Dew — like, half a can — and looked at the words again.

THE GLYPHMASTER AWAITS YOU.

You had no idea who that was?

None. I figured it had to be one of the booger boys. I thought they had to be messing with me. But then I wondered how they would know about the field test. It wasn't like I'd issued an open invitation.

I had surveillance cameras mounted on telephone poles all over the place, and I usually set them up days before a planned event so I could run population scenarios. The cameras could detect movement — cars driving by, people walking past, that sort of thing. Dogs and cats tended to skew the results, but that was built into the code as well. By the time a test location was chosen it had to score no more than a 6.9, which meant that no more than seven total events would occur during the span of an hour. If more than seven cars, baby strollers, or anything else was moving through that space in sixty minutes, the location was scrapped. The last thing we needed was people watching us.

I pulled the data file from one of the Brontobyte drives, which could hold about 28,000 hours of captured footage, and dialed it back to the moment the test began. I could see the card stuck in the door, like a tiny white space on a checkerboard. I set my software to show me each instance where a moving object had entered the screen. I worked backward in time, from the moment Lewis and Emily entered the building. It didn't take long for the white card to disappear.

Ten minutes before the field test a car went by.

Twelve minutes before the field test a cat slinked past.

Twenty minutes before the test a person on a cell phone.

And twenty-seven minutes before our field test, a person — it appeared to be a girl, not a grown woman — walked up to the door, unfolded a stepping stool, and climbed up. She placed the card, turned, and hid her face with her hand.

18:15

Did you recognize her?

I had no idea who she was. None whatsoever.

I could tell immediately, though, that she was smart. She knew the surveillance camera was of the weakest possible quality, especially from a distance. She knew all I'd see was a grainy face with sunglasses on. She folded her stool, picked it up, and walked away as if she didn't have a care in the world.

I was interrupted by a classic Finn moment — him showing up unexpectedly on his monitor in the Vault and looking to be entertained.

"Yo, bro, what are we doing?" he asked, gazing into his camera lens with one eye, huge and searching, which he liked to do as a joke.

I told him he was interrupting my work, but I could never help smiling when he eyeballed me that way. There was something very funny about being stared at like I was in a petri dish.

"Come on," he said. "Play us some Hearts."

I remember looking at my watch. It was already eleven thirty.

"Okay, fine," I told him. "But just one game."

"One's all it's gonna take," Finn said, spinning around in his chair and logging onto our favorite game site. Playing cards would be the easiest way to keep the Trackers distracted while I worked. Emily and Finn made small talk and Lewis was characteristically quiet as the game went on. I toggled back when I had to, but kept my attention on searching for the Glyphmaster.

Why didn't you tell them?

I don't know. It just seemed . . . separate.

Why?

I guess because it had been my symbol. I was the one the Glyphmaster was looking for, not them. What if it had been Google looking for the next big thing? I needed to sniff this thing out on my own, see if it was an opportunity or a threat.

So you lied to your friends.

Not telling them is different from lying. At that point, they didn't need to know.

I refocused on the game site and found Emily and Lewis still typing messages back and forth to each other. They didn't notice my silence. I went back to work.

THE GLYPHMASTER AWAITS YOU.

I just had to see what was there, you know?

No matter what the consequences?

Remember what I said before, about how everyone leaves a trail? In hindsight, this was one of those trails I probably shouldn't have followed. This was the one with the grizzly standing in the shadows, I'll grant you that. But I wasn't thinking about consequences at the time. I was just a curious kid, nothing more.

>> 18:20

I opened a tab over the card game and typed in the only Web address that made any sense, www.Glyphmaster.com. I figured I'd see some sort of message, a joke, or something from one of the booger boys, maybe a guy with his finger up his nose. What I found instead both surprised and delighted me.

The Glyphmaster site was clearly some sort of puzzle. All the symbols we'd come up with were floating around the screen in cloud formations. Some clouds were big, like the group of noun Glyphs all bunched together and slowly circling one another. There were smaller groupings on the screen made up of adjectives and pronouns, adverbs and prepositions, a little burst of conjunctions and articles. I was reminded of earlier heated conversations about the words and wondered who might have organized them this way.

To someone who was outside of our group this strange-looking site would have no meaning whatsoever, but to a person who understood the language, it was like a visual dictionary, something I'd never thought to create.

"Dude, are you playing or working?" Finn said, interrupting my concentration. "This is the slowest game of Hearts in the history of the planet."

I looked at Finn, who was texting someone while he waited for me to make my next move. After a quick scan of the cards left in my hand, I threw out a two of spades.

Finn made the sound of a toilet being flushed, which was to say I was flushing out a certain kind of card, and I went back to the Glyphmaster.

There were ten random Glyph symbols twisting around in the open air. When they entered a cloud they disappeared, then reappeared in the open a few seconds later. I clicked on one of them. It lit up red and exploded, then reappeared once again.

"Cool," I said, getting the hang of it already as I opened up a blank text document and began typing. I typed all ten words represented by the free-falling Glyphs:

much this first the welcome will hard to get level

About ten seconds later I'd already figured out the coded message spelled out in between the clouds of Glyph symbols. I simply changed one of the Glyph's from *hard* to *harder* (a common necessity in the Glyph language) and rearranged the order of the symbols:

Welcome to the first level. This will get much harder.

How did this make you feel?

Excited. Challenged. Totally into it.

But you still insist you had no idea what you were getting yourself into?

I thought it was a puzzle — *only* a puzzle. What was I supposed to think? I had no idea where it would lead.

I heard Finn carrying on and made another move in the card game, trying to stay calm as I clicked on each of the words at the Glyphmaster. When I clicked *welcome* first, it turned green and slid down the page, locking into place at the bottom in one of the empty slots. Each successive symbol turned green and slid into place, until I had all the symbols correctly chosen.

Emily logged onto her screen over my head.

"You're not really into this, are you?" she asked, staring down at me.

"Uh . . . just busy, is all," I said. "Can I fold?"

"There's no folding in Hearts," said Lewis. "It's not poker."

"Game's not as fun with three," Finn added.

Everything on the Glyphmaster screen began to move. I was nervous about missing something important I'd never get to see again. This was a concern I'd long since planned for in the Vault, because the Vault was a place that was full of constant distractions. Trackers video feeds, text messages, Web sites, hardware tests, surveillance footage — it was really humming most hours of the day. Usually this didn't bother me, because I thrived on chaos, but sometimes the solution to a big problem I'd been working on for days crystallized and came clear. When that happened, I needed total silence in the Vault. If I couldn't shut out all the noisy interruptions in a flash, I might lose a brilliant idea forever. I'd actually lost an idea in just that way a couple of years back, when Finn and Emily started arguing over my head at the exact moment I figured out how to make the Trinity camera work. It was like I had it, but then all the parts blew up in my head and had to be put back together like a puzzle. It took weeks to get that idea back again, but it taught me a valuable lesson: Always have an escape plan.

My escape plan consisted of two cords that hung loose from the ceiling like sagging clotheslines. I could reach either one of them if I put my arm over my head and grabbed, sort of like pulling a bell-cord from a seat on a city bus. One of the cords in the Vault was yellow, the other was red.

The yellow cord turned off anything that could distract me: video feeds, surveillance cameras, audio, music. Yellow stopped short of killing my Internet feeds and cutting me off from the outside world entirely, which only happened if I pulled the red cord. Red would shut down all communication in or out, including Web feeds. It was there in the rare case of an emergency, like if I thought someone was attempting to hack past my multiple firewalls or I needed total stillness in the Vault.

Lewis, Emily, and Finn were waiting for me again, all of them staring at me in unison as I reached up from my chair.

I heard Finn yell "Don't pull that cord!" but I ignored him, grabbing the yellow line and yanking down, hearing the hum of activity die instantaneously as all the video screens went dark.

The Glyphmaster remained on the screen right in front of me. The symbols were moving off to the sides of the screen, leaving an empty space in which a black box appeared. A few seconds later, without having to click anything else on the screen, a video started playing.

The screen filled with curtains pulled halfway shut. A space of maybe two feet opened to a dim sky of clouds, a familiar look that reminded me of the late afternoon sky in Seattle. Someone sat in a chair before the window, staring at me.

Light pouring in from the window obscured the face, casting a deep shadow that made any sort of expression hard to perceive. But I knew who it was instantaneously. It was no one I had met before, no one I could have said was part of the Glyph language team. No, this was the same person who had left the card. I knew this not because of her face, because I couldn't really see her clearly either time. I knew it because of the shape of her hair, long and distinctive. It was the same silhouette I'd seen on the street.

She spoke.

What did she say?

Here. I can show you. I still have the video, and I've re-created the Glyphmaster — which disappeared three days later — and posted it at the Trackers interface. If you want to understand everything that happened, to see it as it unfolded, you'll have to stop listening and start watching. I need a break anyway. Give me five and I'll collect my thoughts for round two.

Can I see my friends?

No. But I'll give you the break. What's the password?

Subject Adam Henderson stood, stretched, and asked for an energy drink. Then he turned the laptop in my direction and told me the password.

Note: A transcript of Zara's message is in *Appendix C, page 165.*

www.trackersinterface.com

PASSWORD

BABBAGE424

Video reveals person of interest. Glyphs are also explained further (not in Appendix C). Glyphmaster puzzle in working order, and a list of existing symbols in the Glyph language. More elaborate than I expected.

Adam Henderson continues to relay information in a way I've never encountered before. It really is as if he remembers these things — words, scenes, conversations, weather — exactly as they occurred. If there is such a thing as a videographic memory, Adam Henderson is in possession of it. Note: Check with department psychologist. Is this possible?

What were your first thoughts when you saw the video?

Honestly? I thought, *What kind of name is Zara?*

The video ended, the Glyph symbol clouds rolled in, and Glyphs drifted randomly into open space. It was kind of beautiful, actually, and I sat there mesmerized while my phone began to buzz. Finn or Emily or Lewis, for sure, trying to get my attention. I stared at the flying words, trying to formulate a pattern or a meaning.

Three hours later I fell asleep at my desk, without a hope in the world of figuring out Zara's next puzzle.

So what did you do next?

Next? I worked. Summer was no vacation at Henderson's Chip Shop. As far as my dad was concerned, no school meant he could load me up with a lot more work than he normally would. This reality hit me head-on when I opened the door to the Vault in search of food and a shower the next morning. Blocking my path were piles of hard drives and computer boxes with a note scrawled out in my dad's nearly impossible-to-read handwriting.

These are due tomorrow, better get busy.

I yelled for my dad, walking past the endless array of computers and monitors piled up everywhere. When I reached the front counter he was taking an order from someone, a guy who didn't bother to look up and say hi as they completed their transaction. An early summer rain was falling, and the guy, who was dark-skinned with black hair, unsheathed his umbrella the moment he got outside.

"Another drive for you," I remember my dad saying. He wouldn't do the really boring work of rearranging ones and zeros. He added, "This one looks a little wet, so be extra careful."

Living in a rain-soaked area like Seattle, it was amazing to me how many people ignored the simple fact that water and computers don't mix.

I knew it was hopeless, but I tried to tell my dad that something important had come up. I asked him if I could start on the drives the next day.

"Oh, no, you don't," he said. "I've been holding down the fort for weeks. School's out, which means the *Seattle Times*, a nice cup of coffee, and a Grind House cinnamon roll. Be back in an hour. Don't bug your mother."

I tried to argue the point, but he put his hand up and held it there while he moved toward the door, then drifted out into the rain before I could say another word. I knew if I was extremely lucky he'd be back by lunch and not a minute sooner. I turned the door sign to CLOSED, took the new order, placed it next to the rest of the orders in front of my door, and left in search of breakfast.

Did you feel like you were being watched?

Now that I think back on it, I felt — I don't know, not watched but *guided*, I guess, like I was grabbing for something that was being carefully pulled out of my reach.

So you went looking for breakfast?

Yeah. The nice thing about the shop is that our apartment is upstairs, so getting home was a snap. In fact, there really isn't any distinction between the apartment upstairs and the shop downstairs on the street level. It's all home, and I was just as likely to stay in the shop all night as I was to make the effort to find my room. If someone was watching me from outside at that point, then he or she wouldn't have known if I was upstairs or down, at work or at home.

Anyway, I passed by my mom's study and said good morning, changed clothes and brushed my teeth, made a gargantuan bowl of Froot Loops, and returned to the Vault. An hour later I had seven hard drives on my desk, all of them hooked up to the Vault in one way or another, running endless loops of tests. I had the housing off a printer and a motherboard slotted into a rack getting a new power supply. The front doorbell went off about once every fifteen minutes, signaling the arrival of a customer or — wishful thinking — my dad returning from a lazy morning with the paper.

One of the Vault monitors was trained on the front door so I knew what a customer was bringing in before I met them at the counter. All morning long I ran back and forth between the

Vault and the front of the store, taking in new orders, charging Visas, and handing over finished projects. At noon the door chimed and I looked up, hoping to see my dad, and saw Emily, Finn, and Lewis. Lewis was carrying a pizza box, Finn a bag of what had to be drinks he was sure to spill all over the store if I didn't get him out of Henderson's fast.

I punched a blue button on the Vault wall, a makeshift PA system that kept me in my chair some of the time, and my voice echoed into the front of the store.

"Hey, guys, take it outside," I said. "I'll be right there."

"Let's do this," Finn responded. "I'm starving."

"You're always starving," Emily pointed out. "It's amazing you don't weigh three hundred pounds."

"Skating keeps me trim for the ladies," Finn bragged.

"What ladies?" Emily asked.

"Yeah," added Lewis, "I never see you with any ladies."

Typical friendly banter, nothing out of the ordinary for the Trackers.

Finn ignored them both, and I watched the monitor as they turned for the door. They walked out and I took a quick second to check over all the drives and make sure my software was still doing its job. My stomach rumbled as Lewis came on his Vault screen, eyeing me through the Deckard camera.

"Finn says you better get out here before he eats your two slices," he warned me.

"Don't get grease on that camera," I said. "Remember, it's the only one we have for at least a week."

Lewis made a face like he couldn't believe he'd let the Deckard and a pizza get within a hundred miles of each other, and I headed for the door.

Outside Henderson's is nice — in fact, it's one of my favorite places to hang out, especially when it's raining. We have a wide awning that covers half the sidewalk, a small table, some benches along the storefront. Out there you can watch the world go by and relax. There's a record store, a pizza-by-the-slice, and a lot of cafés. Seattle is crazy about coffee.

"Thanks for the chow, guys," I told everyone. "I'm really under the gun in there. My dad's got me working double time."

"No worries," Finn said as he cracked open a Mountain Dew and handed it to me. "You ditched us at the card table last night, but you're still our fearless leader."

"How are the new cameras working?" I asked, stuffing half a slice of pizza in my mouth.

"The Deckard needs to be synced to the Vault," Lewis explained. "I tried last night but it wouldn't connect."

"I'll do it this afternoon," I said. "We don't have another test scheduled for a few days, so we're okay."

Usually, all the cameras were synced with separate Brontobyte drives in the Vault, making a backup of all the data in case we needed it for anything later.

"I was thinking," Lewis continued. "The Deckard is waterproof to what, forty feet? It was on when I dropped it, so it's probably dead by now. But it's down there in the bay."

"That thing is long gone, probably in the belly of a whale," said Finn.

"We don't have whales in the bay," Emily said. "But the Deckard does have a latent GPS. Maybe we could fish it out somehow."

Emily was referring to the fact that all the camera units worked off a separate, tiny battery system. Even if everything else ran out of juice, the GPS would run for several days in case we lost a unit and needed time to find it. This was a great chance to distract the group for a while so I could work in peace, and I jumped in excitedly.

"Say, you know what? That's not a bad idea. Let's make this into a sort of training mission of its own. The Deckard is worth trying to save, and the GPS data would tell us a lot about its location. Lewis, could you run some tide data and create a map of where it's been in the last twelve hours?"

Lewis lit up with interest. "Sure I could. That'd be easy."

"And Emily, you and Finn could devise some sort of deep-water claw. You're good with motors and mechanics. See what you can do."

"I'm telling you guys, a whale ate it." Finn laughed. "That thing is halfway to China by now."

"Come on, Finn, it'll be fun," said Emily. "The jaws of life — I can already see it."

This seemed to get Finn's attention, so I threw them another bone.

"I tell you what: If you guys can get that camera back, I'll show you my newest invention."

"You don't mean . . . ?" Lewis began to ask.

"You're serious?" added Finn. "You'll finally unveil the Orville?"

I nodded, knowing how much this meant to the Trackers team.

"I might even let you try it," I said.

"Don't let him near it, Adam," said Emily. "If the Orville does what you say it will, it won't last ten seconds with Finn at the controls."

I remember smiling at that. "What can I say?" I told her. "I like to live on the edge. You guys go it alone for today and tomorrow, let me catch up on the work I need to do, and find that camera."

This was perfect. The Trackers would be totally occupied with a mission that would keep them busy, and I could concentrate on the secret thing I wanted to work on: the Glyphmaster.

You didn't think about telling them?

Sure, I thought about telling them what I'd found, the card and the Glyphmaster, but I wasn't sure if someone was watching us or not, and I didn't want to freak them out. Finn would love it, Emily would be full of questions, and Lewis would break out in a cold sweat. I thought it was better to wait, see if it amounted to anything. That's what a good team leader does, right?

So you kept it to yourself?

Yes.

And was that a wise thing to do?

Look, what's the point of second-guessing? I did what I did. I made the choices I made. They felt right at the time.

But if only you'd known . . .

You're not hearing me. There would have been no point in telling them at that point. It was nothing, just an online game. Of course, I might have thought twice if I'd known what would happen. But life doesn't work that way, does it?

Take me back to the Vault, after you left your friends.

The Vault was home to all of my secret inventions. The plans for my mobile devices, tons of software I'd developed for tracking and analyzing data, programs I used to scan and fix computer and hardware problems. I guarded this stuff behind firewalls I'd made myself, because I didn't trust Mr. Gates to protect me from the digital world outside. I'd scoured the Net over the years, finding outdated bank firewalls and security systems. There was a lot out there, floating around like space junk, just waiting to be found and picked clean of any usefulness. I was an expert at taking software apart, adding pieces together, creating new and better systems.

One of the items I'd been working on for almost a year was the Orville, which I refused to show to anyone, not even Emily, Finn, and Lewis. The Orville was my first attempt at a flying reconnaissance unit, and it had to be perfect. I'd had a lot of problems with its weight and its ability to be controlled directly from the Vault, but I'd finally solved the most difficult challenges. In fact, unknown to the rest of the Trackers, all of the surveillance cameras I'd placed during the past year were also remote stations that would carry the Orville signal. There were thirty-one remote stations, all tied into a grid that spanned several miles and tied directly into a wireless router on the roof of our apartment. If I had my calculations right, and I was sure I did, the Orville could take off from Henderson's and fly up to ten miles in any direction with me guiding it via remote control. Everything it saw, I would see, and the video feed would stream into the Vault drives during each flight.

Sometimes I looked around the Vault and thought about all the secret inventions I'd created. The day was coming, or so I thought, when I'd start my own version of Apple and put everything into play. The development, the field tests, the endless streams of data. If I had to guess, it was all worth tens of millions, maybe more.

Of course, there were interruptions. There was the Glyphmaster, which I was obsessing over. And there were my parents, who wanted me to eat food with them around a table like a normal family. I remember my dad peeking into the Vault unexpectedly and saying, "Hey, Mr. Head in the Clouds. What have you got there?"

He was staring at the Glyphmaster, with its spinning, tumbling Glyph images falling from the clouds.

Did you tell him what it was?

No, I said it was just a screen saver I was working on. I told him it was like a game, but I wasn't really sure what it would end up being.

How did he react?

He just nodded and said, "You're freaky smart — you know that, right?"

"Apparently not smart enough to get you to do some of the work around here," I told him.

He laughed and told me it was time for dinner.

Once a week we dropped everything and gathered in the apartment to tell each other what we were doing with our lives, which I realize sounds sort of sad in its brevity, but it totally worked for us. We were actually a very happy family in our own way, before I ended up in here. We were cut from the same cloth, and I liked how we weren't always hounding each other to spend crazy amounts of time together. There was something about the fact that we were all standing or sitting around in the same four thousand square feet that made it feel okay.

I was in for a surprise, though, when I returned to the seclusion of the Vault that night.

The Glyphmaster had changed while I was gone.

What was different?

There was a puzzle to solve.

Wait, I don't understand. Wasn't there always a puzzle to solve? I thought that was the whole point.

You thought wrong and so did I. All those hours staring at the clouds of Glyph symbols floating in groups and it never occurred to me they might be at rest, that there was no puzzle to solve. But this time, when I looked at the screen, some of the symbols had drifted out of the clouds and started falling like snow. They were out in the open, lots of them, and it just made sense. Those Glyphs had to spell out a message.

Fascinating. What were the other Trackers doing while you were locked away in the Vault?

The next day Emily Webcammed in to tell me the progress on the deep dive for the Deckard, but I barely listened to her.

"We think the Deckard is about thirty feet below the surface," she said. "Lewis has narrowed its location to about twenty square feet. And this claw is amazing!"

She was holding a remote control that had once been used for a car or a plane — Emily was really into remote controls — and when she moved one of the swivel sticks, the claw jumped to life.

I had my hand on the yellow cord, dying to focus all of my attention on the Glyphmaster but worried I would hurt Emily's feelings. This was especially true as I watched the claw open and close uncontrollably. Emily backed away and looked like she thought the claw might come after her.

"It's still in beta," she said, trying to get the claw to stop grabbing. "Not as bad as it looks, really. I'm close on this."

She tried to grab it by the arm, but it was jumping around so frantically it nearly chomped into her hand and she yelled, backing away again.

"Look, Emily," I said, "I really have to go. Can we talk about this later?"

"Hang on!" she yelled from somewhere off camera. The next thing I knew a broomstick was bashing the claw over and over until it stopped, its metal fingers sighing open like it had just been killed. Emily leaned into the screen.

"No worries!" she said. "This is in better shape than you probably think. A few hours, that's all I need. Tomorrow morning, we're getting that camera."

"Keep me posted, okay?" I said. "I *really* gotta run. *Totally* backed up over here."

She started to ask if I could join the other Trackers somewhere. But the Glyphmaster was too enticing and I finally had to pull the yellow cord. I felt terrible cutting Emily off like that, but I'd seen something in the puzzle that made my mind jump to life just like the claw had done. It was the same as before, the falling symbols grouping into the clouds, some of the symbols hanging in the sky.

There were two things that struck me as I opened a text file and began typing out words. The first was that some of the Glyphs were symbols I'd never seen before. These were symbols that had been made by someone else, not me or anyone from the old group, so at first glance I shouldn't have known what they represented. But I did know what they were meant to say, because the second thing that struck me was that this was a message I'd heard before.

There were thirty-five symbols to order, which should have looked like a near-impossible task, but it wasn't impossible at all. I went online, typed in a search for a certain name, just to be sure. And there it was.

I had long been subjected to quotes by my mother, who'd spent the past few years working on a book about explorers. You see, explorers are notoriously quote worthy, and she kept a logbook of every famous explorer saying she'd come across over the years and sometimes read them while we ate her crunchy rice and chicken dish. There were hundreds if not thousands of quotes, and she kept them meticulously organized. Sometimes I would peak into the logbook on her desk and read through the more interesting ones. And this one, the quote I'd just typed out, was a phrase I'd heard my mother say more recently than I was comfortable with. Seeing it there on the page made me feel uneasy.

Here — I can show you the symbols I saw, with the ones I needed circled.

Subject went to computer and loaded up a list of symbols, then circled certain ones. I have placed it in Appendix D, page 167.

So what do the symbols mean?

Isn't it obvious?

You're joking, right?

Sorry. Couldn't help myself. This is the quote they represent:

The church says the earth is flat, but I know that it is round, for I have seen the shadow on the moon, and I have more faith in the shadow than in the church.

It may strike you as odd that I would remember such a lengthy quote, but this was a Magellan quote, and there was a funny thing about Magellan: Unlike most explorers, he was highly *un*quotable. In fact, that quote is the *only* one he's known for, one my mother has said many times over the past two years as she worked on her book.

I have always been a steady guy at the keyboard, even when I was juiced on way too much caffeine and my fingers were flying as I typed out a line of code. But my hand was shaking on the mouse as I clicked on each symbol and watched them fall quickly into place. Whoever this Glyphmaster was, she knew more about my family than I was comfortable with.

You didn't think the Magellan quote was a coincidence?

No way. Impossible.

So what happened when you clicked on the images?

As soon as I ordered the words perfectly, a second video appeared.

It was the girl again. Zara. I still couldn't see what she looked like, her face obscured by the shadows and backlight from the window, but she appeared a little clearer now as she spoke.

Here. I'll show you the video. It's in the interface under a new password. And you can see the new Glyphmaster puzzle solved, too. I rebuilt it.

Note: A transcript of Zara's message is in Appendix E, page 169.

www.trackersinterface.com

PASSWORD

SAMLOYD127

Was there anything else besides the message?

Nope. And the Glyphmaster went back to its resting state, where no puzzle could be found. Just the cloud formations again, nothing else.

So Zara knew your name. She knew where you all liked to hang out.

It was eerie. I knew it had to be someone I'd associated with before — either that, or I hadn't been careful enough protecting my own identity. The whole thing was starting to make me nervous as I reached for the mouse, but I stopped just short of shutting the Glyphmaster down.

You couldn't help yourself.

The thought of meeting Zara in person was . . . well, it was definitely something I was interested in. She was smart, mysterious, beautiful. How could I *not* want to meet her? I let the Glyphmaster sit there, doing its dance, just in case Zara came back.

The clock ticked past eight and I stared at the drives and computers piled up on my desk. I still had a lot of work to do before I could even think about taking a break. One of the drives had turned out to be unrepairable; another needed more attention. And the wet one brought in by that guy? That drive was giving me all sorts of fits. It kept acting like it was fixed, then going all haywire again every time I disconnected it from the Vault. There's nothing like water to disrupt an otherwise healthy technological ecosystem.

As the night wore on, I kept a close eye on the Glyphmaster and began running IP address searches to see if I could locate where the site was hosted. If I could figure that out, it might give me a clue that would help me find this mysterious Zara person. I felt sure the whole thing had to be tied to someone I'd worked with in the past, someone from the old group, so I started sending out messages to people who'd been a part of the Glyph language team, asking them if they knew of any recent activity.

Everyone came back with the same answer: nothing. Which is not to say someone wasn't lying. The truth was, I hadn't even met any of them and didn't know what most of them looked like. For all I knew Zara was pretending to be a zit-faced, *Halo*-addicted dude when we were working on the Glyph.

She could have been anyone.

Anyone. Anywhere. But I knew one thing for sure: Zara was near enough to know me. She was near enough to be watching.

19:07

I stayed up until after midnight and didn't allow any of the Trackers entrance into the Vault. Instead, I put all my effort into fixing every single project my dad had given me, doing all the paperwork, and setting everything on the completed shelves out front. I even made it to my own bed upstairs and had a bowl of cereal with my mom and dad the next morning. By the time I got downstairs it was almost ten, and my dad was nodding his head appreciatively at the pile of orders I'd finished.

"I hate to break the bad news to you," he said.

I knew where this was going. I didn't want him to say it.

But he said it anyway, with an ominous look of death. "*They* called. Which means you're about to get very busy."

"I just did, like, seven orders in one night!" I protested.

"Hey, I can't help when Microsoft calls; they just do. And I can't help it when they drive that beautiful white Microsoft van up to my door with — what was it last time? Was it thirty-eight computers that needed fixing?"

I told him I remembered it was thirty-nine.

He went on and reminded me it was serious money in the bank — money we needed.

Those big Microsoft orders only happened about three times a year, but whenever they came in, we scrambled for days on end. This was on top of the usual stuff, which wasn't exactly slow as far as I could tell. I felt like I'd blown off my friends for an entire day or more, there was the Glyphmaster, and now this? Microsoft, the biggest technology company in the world, was about to gobble up my entire week.

"I'll order in pizza," said my dad. "We'll tag team the whole batch, shouldn't take us more than a few days. Unless it's like that one time . . ."

I told him not to remind me.

My dad's eyes lit up like cash registers at the thought of our biggest Microsoft order ever: forty-three computers, seven printers, and twelve random hard drives. In classic Microsoft fashion they wanted it all fixed and ready to be picked up in one week. It was the first time I pulled an all-nighter. My dad even let me skip school so I could work.

You needed money that badly?

Hey, everybody needs money. Wait — I don't mean it that way. I don't want you thinking money is all I cared about.

I didn't say that.

But I know how it sounds. Nothing that happened was because of money. I can see you don't believe me — but it's true.

I'm trying to believe you.

You know what? Think whatever you want. The point is my dad needed big orders to stay afloat. The shop needed the work.

So the order came in and you were stuck. How did that go?

I remember my dad unlocked the front door and peered down the street, undoubtedly searching for the Microsoft van that would bring dozens of broken computers his way and destroy my social life.

"Nothing yet," he told me. "You're in the clear for the moment."

I bolted for the Vault as fast as my legs would carry me, away from any new customers or duties my dad might make me take care of. I might have ten minutes or two hours, but I at least had to get in contact with Emily and let her know I'd probably have to miss seeing her put the claw to use in the Deckard rescue attempt.

I was just about to fire up all the monitors and check in with the whole crew when I glanced at the Glyphmaster and saw that it had changed yet again. A new puzzle had arrived, shorter this time, with more custom Glyphs.

One was a peace sign, another an eyeball. I lowered slowly into my chair with my fingers already tapping against the mouse.

"I know this message," I whispered out loud. "It can't be right."

But it was. I turned around in my chair, rolling back a few feet, and faced the corkboard that served as a place to hold incoming paperwork. In the bottom right corner, wedged there for as long as I'd had the Vault, was that picture from Old Henderson, my grandfather. It was stuck there backward, so I could see his handwriting whenever I wanted to. The black-and-white picture of the stream was facedown, which always struck me as poetic given the words my grandfather had left behind:

The hardest thing to find is peace, though it lay in plain view.

This was the solution to the Glyphmaster puzzle? A penciled line of words from my mountain man grandfather? But how? I'd never said those words to anyone. The only people who could know about them, as far as I could tell, were my parents and anyone who had been in the Vault. It was the only time I ever imagined, for an instant, that one of the Trackers might be messing with me. Who else could it be? They were the only ones I'd let this far into my world. They were the only ones who could know about what Old Henderson had written on the back of that picture.

I was suddenly very uncomfortable with what was happening. Whoever this Zara person was, she knew way more than I could have ever imagined. The only way she could know about this picture was if she'd seen it for herself, and that could only happen if she'd seen the inside of the Vault.

My dad's voice came over the Vault intercom.

"The big guys just called. They won't be here for another hour. I'm heading for the Grind House, be back in thirty."

I heard the bell ring out front and looked into the surveillance camera.

"I'll get that, you rest up for the show," said my dad.

The guy with the wet hard drive had returned, this time without an umbrella since the weather had cleared.

My eyes locked on the Glyphmaster, but I wasn't sure what I should do. If I solved the puzzle, what then? Was I telling Zara something I shouldn't be? Maybe I should pull the red cord, lock down the Vault in case she was trying to find something. I couldn't help but wonder: What had she seen besides Old Henderson's postcard?

19:17

I toggled to a different set of Web results and found that the Glyphmaster had a strange series of IP addresses, some of which I had already been able to exclude. She was running an address mirror, which made it incredibly hard to locate the source of the site. I had narrowed it from twenty-five to six, but the six were all over the place. One put the site at a hosting service in Texas, another in Sweden, two more in Russia, one in California, and one in Portland, closest to my neck of the woods. And, really, any of these could be a front for Seattle — the miracle and curse of the Internet was that Seattle could connect just as easily to Russia as it could to Portland.

I'd hammered away at the site location as best I could, but my software couldn't break the code. This girl Zara was smart. *Very* smart.

Against my better judgment I opened the lines of communication on the Vault. Exactly four seconds later, Lewis appeared on his screen.

"You better run if you don't want to be found," he said. "Emily and Finn are on their way to Henderson's."

This was just what I *didn't* need right at the moment. I guessed I had only a few seconds before one of them called in from the street, because there was no way of hiding once communication was re-established. The Trinity and the Belinski would blink green for the Vault, and they'd know I was back online.

I asked Lewis for an update on Emily's claw project, and he told me she'd gotten it dialed in. He thought it was going to work, but it would depend on whether or not he'd gotten the location for the Deckard correct. The tides were soft in the bay, but they still wreaked havoc with his spreadsheets.

I felt a little bit guilty for making them go to so much trouble on a mission whose only real purpose was to keep them busy. I felt sure it was beyond impossible to find a sunken camera.

"They pushed back the time so they could come find you, but I gotta run," Lewis said to me. "With or without you, we go in forty-five minutes."

I told him I wouldn't be there, but asked him to film the mission for me. He promised he would.

Lewis signed off and I took another scan of the monitors. The street was humming with cars outside, the dark-haired guy was paying my dad in cash and getting ready to leave, and the Glyphmaster puzzle was staring back at me, wanting to be solved.

"Where have you been?" a voice suddenly asked.

I looked up and there was Emily, staring at me as she rode her mountain bike along the street.

"Keep your eyes on the road," I told her. "Lots of cars out there."

I was happy to see that she wasn't too cool to wear a helmet.

"It's all good, we talked to your dad," Finn piped in. He was holding on to the back of Emily's bike, being pulled along on his skateboard.

"Yeah, sorry about the news," said Emily. "It would have been great to have you there."

"I'm just glad you understand," I said, feeling a sudden burst of goodwill for my peeps.

"Hey, when Microsoft calls, you have to listen," Emily said, smiling into the wind. "We'll broadcast so you can see what we're doing. The claw rules!"

"Yeah!" yelled Finn. "Beware the claw!"

They were both laughing, and I wished more than anything that I could join the Trackers at the warehouse for some deep-sea diving.

"Signing off for now," said Emily. "Don't work too hard, 'kay?"

"I won't," I lied. "And be careful — don't fall into the bay."

The monitors went dead and I knew they were saving battery power for the field test. I felt better about having set it up for them, because it helped me see they'd really become a team.

"Okay, Glyphmaster, time to die," I vowed.

You were determined?

Yeah. I had to crack the thing. You have to understand — I was used to cracking whatever was put in front of me. So the fact that I hadn't figured this out yet was driving me crazy — as much as the feeling of being watched was freaking me out. And besides that, I knew the answer. I had determined there was more to be gained by filling in the blanks than cutting off communication with this thing.

So what did you do?

I grabbed the floating Glyph symbols one by one and watched them click into place. It was eerie seeing my grandfather's quote take shape in a game that might be hosted in one of six places around the world.

THE HARDEST THING TO FIND IS PEACE, THOUGH IT LAY IN PLAIN VIEW.

The screen cleared, just as it had done before, only this time there was no video. Instead a new message, written in Glyph, arranged itself in front of me.

I WANT TO SEE YOU, it said.

There was a break in the line of symbols, representing a pause, and then one more word:

SOON.

19:23

I stared at the screen, trying to imagine what in the world was going on with this game I'd been immersed in for days. Or even if it was a game at all. What sort of twisted trick was this Zara person trying to pull? First she hijacked my language for her stupid game, then she started digging into my personal life, and now this — I didn't know what — this leading message. The worst part was that I was still totally intrigued. Part of me was like, yeah, this girl gets me. And she's hot. That would be the stupid part of me. The other part of me, the not-brainless part, was hearing alarm bells ring from one side of the Vault to the other.

The intercom jumped to life and I heard my dad's voice.

"Hey there, the guy with the wet drive wanted me to tell you thanks, you have no idea what you've done for him."

I pressed the intercom button.

"I hope you told him to stay out of the rain. That was a tough one."

"Twenty-seven minutes to D-Day. Keep resting. I need my heavyweight champ for the full twelve rounds. Mountain Dew is on the way — Mom's on it."

I could only imagine the amount of junk that was about to show up on the front counter. What if it was a new record, like fifty computers? I'd be out of commission for days, maybe a whole week.

But the Glyphmaster couldn't wait.

I stared at the monitors: still no Emily, Finn, or Lewis. I opened another browser and searched for Zara, found nothing remotely interesting, then I figured I better get organized for the onslaught. I usually ran a cleanup protocol after a long night, which drifted through my entire system looking for anything weird or out of sync. In the early days there were lots of spyware programs that glommed on to my software like leeches, harmless other than to slow things down. I'd long since solved that kind of problem with firewalls and screening tests, but still, I liked a tidy environment after a lot of work had been put through the pipeline. Software had a way of tangling up like computer cords if I didn't stay on top of it.

Each bay was hardwired into the Vault so I could review everything in detail, run the programs I needed to, and watch for blips that might tell me what was going wrong with a given piece of hardware. I had used all seven repair bays the night before, so I'd also run cleanup across the board.

The first four bays tested back clean, but the fifth one had some alerts I hadn't seen in a long time. The report showed an alert every time the unit was unplugged from the bay, which it appeared I'd done six different times during the night. I'd plugged and unplugged dozens of pieces of hardware for hours on end. Some of them were USB ports, others were pin-based connections or power supply related. I pulled up a more detailed view of all six alerts and realized that they were all related to the same piece of hardware from the night before. Drilling down into the report, I saw something alarming.

Every one of the alerts was from the wet hard drive, the one that had been brought in the morning before. I recalled how every time I unplugged it from the bay it went dead on me again or started acting up. So I'd plug it back in, reconfigure it, run more tests. On the sixth try it held and I placed it into receiving as fixed.

What I realized now was that this was no ordinary drive, and it hadn't been falling apart on me every time I'd unplugged it. No, this drive had been on a mission. It wasn't just me sending software to it, trying to fix up a mess. The drive had been sending signals into the Vault, looking for things.

This was bad. It meant I'd been hacked, something that I'd never let happen before. I'd been so distracted by the Glyphmaster, by the Trackers, by a pretty girl — I'd let my guard down and something terrible had happened.

The Vault had been infiltrated.

Do you need to stop? Are you hungry?

No. Let's do this.

For the next five minutes my fingers flew over the keys as I searched for where it had been and what it had seen. My findings were not encouraging.

My plans for the Deckard, the Trinity, the Belinski: all hacked.

All my secret programs for fixing hard drives and computers: hacked.

The traces I'd been running: hacked.

My tracker history: vulnerable, if not hacked.

The Orville, not even out of the Vault yet: hacked!

As I was figuring out the damage, my dad piped in with a "Hey, Mr. Heavyweight Champ, your shipment arrives. Looks like a monster! Get those bays ready to roll."

I didn't know what to tell him. So I kept quiet.

What do you think would have happened if you'd told him?

Are you kidding? He would've blown his top. But that's not really why I didn't tell him.

It was still your secret.

Yeah. And *my* problem. I felt if I'd messed it up, I could also find a way to fix it.

I jumped out of my chair and locked the door to the Vault.

I was hyperventilating while I ran through the security archives for the store and found the place where the man had dropped off the wet hard drive. He had dark hair and olive skin — he could've been Italian or Indian or Greek or anything, really. No distinguishing features. I mean, I'd been praying for a birthmark in the shape of *I'm Your Man*, but that wasn't meant to be. He could've been one of a million guys.

I fast-forwarded to the morning where he came in and picked it up. He never looked directly into the camera, but I could see him well enough. Big nose, dark brows, that head of thick black hair.

I went to real-time mode and saw with dread the computers piling up on the counter. There were at least twenty already, and my dad was still heading out for more with the driver. I went back to the reports, sifting through data, trying to find a clue. Whoever this dark-haired man was, he was brilliant. He'd used hacks I'd never seen before, working his way around all my firewalls and taking everything. My inventions had been stolen out from under me, and my tracking technique had been pilfered. I was completely vulnerable. It was a disaster.

I was just about to call Emily, Finn, and Lewis, give them the incredibly bad news, when I saw something else that didn't belong. At the very end of my reports there was always a listing of anything that had been found in the Vault that hadn't been there before. Sometimes a tiny bit of spyware would slip through, then it would get zapped, but its tiny presence would be noted. At the very end of the bay four report, a file was listed with a link to its location. This file was still there, whatever it was, infecting my system.

"We hit the mother lode!" my dad yelled into the intercom. I recall the driver laughed along with my dad.

I clicked on the link, which took me to a video file located deep in a hidden folder on one of my Brontobyte drives. A needle in a haystack.

What I saw on that video file has to be seen to be believed.

Note: A transcript of the footage here is in Appendix F, page 171.

www.trackersinterface.com

PASSWORD

WOZ14

-10 -20 -30 -40 -50 -60 -70 -80 -90 -100

>> 19:42

I should have known Zara was in on the heist from the beginning. The third video made that abundantly clear. How could I have been so dense? First the guy with the hard drive, he called himself Lazlo, he shows up all happy about hacking into my Vault and taking my secrets. Then he turns serious, like I better listen and do as I'm told. As long as I don't call the police he won't leak all my stuff onto the Net so any two-bit programmer can take it for their own. And then he tells me that not only did I have to stay quiet, I have to do whatever he asks.

How did this make you feel?

Helpless. And stupid. *Really* stupid. Because if I hadn't kept cracking those Glyphs, they would have left me alone. In some twisted way, I'd brought this on myself.

You felt guilty?

More like *used*. The Zara part was a shocker, something I didn't see coming. Right from the start of the third video there was something familiar about the room, but I couldn't put my finger on what it was. It wasn't until the camera panned and she came into view that I realized the two of them had been working together the whole time. Chances were she and Lazlo had been planning this for a lot longer than I thought. More than likely, they were part of the original Glyph language team, using false names like everyone else, searching for smart programmers they could rip off.

So, yeah, I was in shock. I was watching the videos over and over and my dad was pounding on the door to the Vault, wondering why I wasn't helping him catalogue all the new work that had just been dumped in my lap.

"I'll start piling things in front of your door," he called out to me. "Watch the paperwork, right? You know how they are, no paper trail, no payment."

I heard my dad drop something heavy and head back to the front of the store for more orders. Rolling the surveillance cameras again, I watched as Lazlo took the hard drive out the front door. Everything I'd ever invented was on that drive, every code I'd ever cracked, and it had slipped away.

I went back to the Glyphmaster Web address. It was gone — totally evaporated, no trace that the site had ever existed to begin with. It was a good thing I'd mirrored the entire thing, code and all, on one of the Vault drives. At least I could continue looking for clues.

I moved all the evidence I had to the Trackers interface, pulled down most of what had been there before, and dialed the whole team at one time. Within seconds I had a visual from Lewis's camera, his face up close in the camera. He was in the warehouse where the Deckard had been lost.

"The claw didn't take too well to water," Lewis stammered. "It sort of, I don't know, exploded, I guess. Emily's not too happy about it. Finn brought a fishing pole."

"Sounds like a disaster," I said, even while I was thinking it wasn't anything compared to the other catastrophe on my hands.

"It doesn't look promising," Lewis reported.

"Gather everyone around," I said. "There's something I need to tell you."

So this was when you finally told them?

Yes.

Why?

Because I realized I'd been a fool to try to do everything on my own. Because I trusted them. Because I wanted to track Zara and Lazlo, and I knew I couldn't do it alone.

Were you worried about their safety?

No. I thought I was the only one in danger. I had no idea what was about to happen.

Did they doubt you?

Not at all. Emily and Finn came in close so I had all three of them staring into the Vault from one camera. I explained everything as fast as I could. The Glyphmaster, the hard drive, Lazlo and Zara, the whole terrible situation.

Finn responded first. "Dude that is *so* cold," he said. "I can't believe it. We gotta take this Lazlo guy down."

"Why didn't you tell us sooner?" Emily pleaded. "We could have been on an actual case, not dredging the bay for a lost camera."

"I hear you," I said. "I definitely should have brought you guys in, but I didn't know about the hack until, like, five minutes ago. I'm just as surprised as you are."

I explained about the meeting Zara had requested. True to her earlier promise, the third video had been clear about what would happen next: She'd meet me at the Grind House at two o'clock tomorrow.

Finn popped his face into the camera. "Holy cow, she's that close? Freaky."

"Who knows?" I continued. "Maybe they're bluffing and they've already left the country. I've uploaded everything to the Trackers interface. You guys get in there and start digging around, see what you can figure out. And start planning for some serious surveillance at the café tomorrow. If Zara or Lazlo show up, we need to be ready."

"This is incredible!" Finn yelled. "A *real* undercover case!" He *loved* this kind of thing. He was the hero in his own mental spy movie, jumping off speeding trains, wrestling with gators, skydiving to get the bad guy. He ate it up.

Lewis, on the other hand, was nervous. "I'm not so sure this is a good idea," he said. "What if it gets dangerous? Someone could get hurt."

In Lewis's mind the someone who could get hurt was always . . . Lewis. He was certain of it.

If Finn was extreme in going for it, and Lewis was extreme in worrying about it, Emily was right down the middle. Levelheaded. Even-keeled. I knew she'd cast the deciding vote.

"No, this is good," she said. "We're more than ready. In fact, we've been ready for a long time. Zara and Lazlo are going to be sorry they messed with the Trackers."

I'll admit — I liked the sound of that.

I heard the claw bounce to life somewhere behind them and Finn ran back, stomping down on the arm.

"No worries!" yelled Finn. "We got this!"

I explained that I needed to work double time all day and

night just to get my dad to cut me loose, and even then, it would be a stretch for him to let me stay out very long.

"You want me to come help you?" asked Lewis. "Those Microsoft guys can really mess up a system. You could be in for a long haul."

"I'd rather you hit the interface and start digging around," I told him. "Maybe you'll see something I missed. I need new eyeballs on everything."

Emily piped in as Finn came back holding the busted claw.

"We're not going to let this happen, Adam. You'll see."

Emily was right. It had only ever been fun and games from the beginning, like a bunch of kids on a playground. For the first time in the three-year history of the Trackers, we were going to see if all our preparation and all my inventions added up to anything in the real world. This time we had a real assignment where the stakes were incredibly high.

This time, it was personal.

With everyone on board, I felt a new surge of energy and excitement about the whole crazy situation. Everything was on the line and maybe, just maybe, we could track Zara and Lazlo before it was too late.

Seventeen hours, two pizzas, and eleven Mountain Dew Code Reds later, I'd pulled an all-nighter and delivered a new record: twenty-four Microsoft computers repaired and ready for delivery. My dad had completed seventeen himself, a huge number for a perfectionist like him, and we were staring at a counter full of finished work. Forty-one computers, all of them with different problems that Microsoft hadn't been able to solve themselves, and all of them fixed.

"Mr. October," said my dad, "you delivered like it was the World Series. By my calculation, this is over ten thousand dollars for the shop. That's a new one-day record."

My dad was motivated by cold hard cash more than ever. With the rising cost of rent and a crummy economy, that amount of money in one day was a big deal at Henderson's Chip Shop.

"You did good," I said, only half joking. Somewhere around midnight it had become like a race to see who could finish boxes first, and before we knew it, my dad and I were watching the sun come up. By eight, we were wrapping up the last few boxes, giddy at the prospect of finishing what should have taken four or five days.

"Old Henderson would have been very proud," Dad said, turning all nostalgic on me. "He always did love a challenge."

We made a deal to keep the store open: I would stay awake until noon and open the doors at nine; my dad would sleep for a few hours, then relieve me of duty. I was twitching with energy, a rush that sometimes overtook my body when I hadn't slept in a long time, but I knew I was likely to crash at some point. I could make it into the afternoon, no problem, but after that, I'd have to turn in early or face a serious bodily shut down.

I returned to the Vault and positioned the camera view of the storefront on the center monitor so I could keep a close eye on things. The Vault was trashed, loose parts and pop cans all over the floor. I picked up a half-eaten slice of cheese pizza and ate breakfast while tidying up the place. The Trackers had checked in off and on until about midnight, relaying plans that were underway, but I hadn't heard from anyone for a while. I guess I was the only one who'd neglected to get some sleep.

At around ten thirty, Emily reported in.

"How's the order coming along?" she asked. "Will your dad spring you?"

I said, "I worked all night, but I'm charged and ready to go. I'm cut loose at noon. What's the update from the field?"

"I can't find Finn," she said. "And Lewis is getting cold feet."

"We both know where Finn is," I told her, and then we both said in unison: "Sleeping."

Emily said she'd talk to Lewis, to make sure he was on board. "This kind of thing is good for him," she said.

"I don't know," I said. "Sometimes I think his heart is going to explode."

"He'll be fine," Emily assured me. "I have a feeling he's going to bring his A game when it matters."

"What else you got for me?" I asked.

"Well, we moved in two of your surveillance boxes like you asked, so we've got views leading to the café from both directions. Finn told me he would add a third, on Fifth, so we could see if anyone walked up that way. He didn't check in on that, so I don't know if it got done. We've tested positions on the street and inside the café, and we think we're covered. If they show up, we should be able to follow them."

I pulled up the three camera boxes that had been moved to run some tests. Two of them were showing grainy views of the Grind House, but the third, the one Finn has been responsible for, was staring straight into the leaves of a tree.

"Looks like we're only going to have two cameras," I told Emily. "Finn's is going to be useless."

"Why am I not surprised?" she replied.

"Daylight now, so we can't move it. We'll have to put a body on Fifth in case they come or go from that direction."

I picked up a half-drank, flat can of pop and washed down a crust of pizza.

"I hope you're planning to brush your teeth before you leave," Emily said.

I nodded and smiled, and Emily said she'd go by Finn's house and rouse him, then gather the team at noon for a run-through.

A few minutes after Emily signed off, Lewis signed onto his monitor eating a Pop-Tart.

"The Glyphmaster is cool," he said. "Very advanced programming with the formations and all."

"Yeah, they know what they're doing, that's for sure," I said.

"It was hosted here in Seattle, you got that, right?" Lewis asked.

I hadn't been sure, but Lewis never made a statement like that unless he'd figured it out.

I asked him how he knew, since I could only narrow it to six places and then got no further.

"I've got it pinpointed to one of three locations, all of them within about ten miles of Henderson's."

Lewis proceeded to explain that he'd found three different slices of code in the overall scheme. It was common for all programmers to cut and paste when they needed different features to work, then string lines of code together and add their own parts in between.

"You're not the only programmer on the team," said Lewis. "I just don't talk about it much, being modest and all."

"Very funny," I told him. "So how'd you do it?"

"It's easy to find the sections that are spliced in, and there were three in the Glyphmaster. I created a search protocol that would take those sections of code and search for matches across the Net. So basically I didn't search for the stuff on the surface of the Internet, I searched the underlying guts. All three splices of code came back in Seattle."

"Lewis," I said, "you're a genius."

"Tell me about it" was his reply.

"But they could have taken those sections of code from anywhere, couldn't they?"

"Nope. Most places tag their code if it gets used by someone else, and these three, they're tagged as local."

Amazing. What Lewis was saying, in simple terms, was that the Glyphmaster was hosted simultaneously at three locations right here in Seattle. Code didn't lie.

I said, "The fact that Lazlo was in Henderson's himself and you've found these code splices means they had to be working out of Seattle. Maybe they'll actually show up today."

"Yeah, about that part," said Lewis, biting down on a corner of the Pop-Tart. "I'm not sure I'm ready for prime time."

"Lewis, you're ready," I assured him. "We all are."

"What makes you so sure?" he asked.

I thought about what I should say. Lewis *had* to be there. He was part of the team and we needed him. Lewis and I had been friends a long time, and I knew the idea of an authentic surveillance mission had redlined his nerves. Field tests had always rattled him, but this was a whole new level.

"At some point all the training has to be for some reason besides playing a game or gathering data. And you owe it to yourself to be there."

"I don't know, couldn't I just stay in the Vault and monitor things from there? Or what about the police? We have Lazlo and Zara on tape; we could let the cops handle this."

I agree with Lewis. Why not let the cops handle it?

Because of Lazlo's threat. All it would take is one click of a button and poof — everything we'd worked on would be floating around on the Net where anyone could take it. We couldn't risk that, not if we had a chance of catching Lazlo and Zara.

I told this to Lewis, too. He slurped at a glass of milk and wiped his hand across his face.

"You really think Zara is in on this?" he asked. "Maybe she's a pawn. Maybe she was trapped in the same way you were."

I hadn't given it that much thought, although I did have to admit I was having a difficult time getting her out of my mind.

"You like her, don't you?" said Lewis. "You're kind of excited to meet her."

"Maybe — I don't know," I said, which was about as close to the truth as I could get.

"Just remember, in the movies, it's always the mysterious hottie who gets the guy in trouble in the end," Lewis warned. "She's supersmart and totally gorgeous, what programmer could resist? I think those things are by design, part of their plan to get you under their spell."

“You see there!” I said. “I need someone to protect me from myself, and that’s you.”

Lewis stared at his desk, took out a pencil, and wrote something I couldn’t see. Then he looked back up at me.

“I’ll be there,” he said.

“I knew I could count on you,” I said, more excited than ever about what we were about to embark on. “We’re all meeting at noon for a run-through. Let’s track these guys down and get back what’s rightfully ours.”

As luck would have it, the Microsoft driver showed up five minutes before I was supposed to leave. There was no way I could get out of reviewing the work I'd done with the driver, and I sure wasn't getting out of my share of loading up the van. Adults had a way of seeing a young, healthy back and immediately loading it down with junk.

Emily had gotten Finn out of bed and Lewis had overcome his jitters — now it was up to me to show up for the most important mission of my life. I raced back to the Vault, told Emily what was going on, and put her in charge. Then I returned to the front of the store where my dad was going through the billing.

It took almost an hour to review everything, and loading the van sapped almost all the energy I had left. After that my dad forced me to go upstairs in search of fresh clothes and a toothbrush. He suggested I pack it in for the day, get some sleep, but he didn't force me to stay in the apartment. A stairwell connected the upstairs to the downstairs, and I didn't squander any time putting myself back together again.

"No more time in the Vault until tomorrow, got it?" he said when I came back down and ran for the door. "You need a break from the hardware."

I didn't have time to argue, so I waved and kept right on going. If I walked fast, I could be at the Grind House by one forty, still twenty minutes to spare. To be on the safe side, I fired up the Roadrunner, threw on my skull bucket, and jumped the curb. Three minutes later I pulled up silently to the curb and parked the scooter.

What were you feeling at this time?

I just wanted it to be over, you know? It was killing me, not knowing what would happen next. I wasn't even sure if Zara would show. For all I knew, it was a trap.

But you went anyway.

What choice did I have, really? This was the only lead we had. And I was hoping that there was strength in numbers — Zara and Lazlo might be expecting me, but they couldn't know that the other Trackers were going to be there, too.

So what did you find when you got there?

Lewis and Emily were waiting for me, sitting at one of the sidewalk tables. Finn was nowhere in sight.

"There you are," said Emily. "We were getting worried you might leave us out here to die."

I explained the delay and asked where Finn was.

"He's inside, talking to the waitress," Lewis said.

I went into the café and found Finn chatting up a cute girl working the counter. All I could think of was here we were, on our most important assignment yet, and Finn was goofing off.

"Mind if I talk to you outside?" I asked.

Finn whirled around, skateboard in hand.

"My man!"

He looked me up and down, saw how tired I was, and tried to impress the girl with his wit.

"Run for your lives, it's *Night of the Living Dead*," he joked.

I wasn't laughing. "Finn, outside, now," I told him.

He tossed a five on the counter and looked back at the girl. "Draw me up a coffee with two extra shots," he said to her. "Caffeine for the zombie, on me."

The girl laughed, Finn laughed, and I turned for the door.

There was no sign of Zara or Lazlo. I even checked to see if someone else was watching — there was no guarantee that this was only a two-person operation on their side. But the café wasn't crowded, and nobody was really paying any attention to me or Finn.

I took this as a good sign.

"Whoa, slow down, Adam, I'm coming," Finn called out. I heard him pull the five back and start following. "Hold that coffee," he told the waitress. "I'll be back."

When we got outside I looked at my watch. 1:42 P.M. It didn't feel like an undercover op, it felt like any other day, like we had no idea what we were doing. It was time to play bad cop as I stood in front of the Trackers.

"Finn," I said, "this is serious business for once. I need you to *engage*."

Finn looked like I'd just knocked his ice cream cone onto the pavement. "That's cold, man," he said. "Really cold. You know I'm ready to roll when it's go time."

"We needed you last night," I pointed out. "That's all I'm saying. That camera placement was important and we're stuck with a superb view of a bird sitting in a tree. It won't do us a lot of good if Lazlo or Zara use Fifth Street."

Finn held up his hands. "I know, I know. Totally my bad. You know how I am after midnight."

"That's no excuse," Emily chimed in. "You're our weak link right now. If we're going to be a team, we have to be able to depend on each other."

This was the thing about being a team leader that Emily had the hardest time understanding. Everyone, including her, had baggage the whole team had to carry around. Finn was so laid-back, some days I thought the guy might melt right into the pavement. And he was terrible after midnight. His concentration went completely out the door. Lewis was nervous and he over-examined every little thing. And Emily? She had a real blind spot when it came to the fact that she could sometimes be critical in a way that didn't help matters.

The cool thing for me as I looked at this amazing group of friends was that I saw the hidden value in their flaws. Emily *was* critical, but without her we'd never get anything done — she was the taskmaster we needed. Lewis, I knew, would never let us get into a jam without first making sure we understood the risks. And Finn? Finn took the edge off of everything stressful, a huge advantage in a group full of brainiacs.

"All right, look," I began. "We've got fifteen minutes to get into position. Let's stay focused on the work we have to do to get this right. If we're lucky and they show up, we're only going to get one shot at this. We all have to do our part. And you guys have to trust me on this, you're ready. None of us is perfect; we all have shortcomings. But together, as a team, we're unstoppable."

Emily nodded slowly, like she'd understood something about Finn maybe she hadn't before.

"You're right," she said. "And we're going to catch them today. I can feel it."

"One other thing," I added. "You're all trained for things to change up on you. Be prepared for it, stay cool under pressure."

I gave Emily the floor and she quickly went over the plan one last time, including our positions. I was to sit in the Grind House at a table in the back balcony, while Finn would sit at the window and keep an eye on the front door. Emily was a few doors down, watching for an approach, and Lewis was on the corner of Fourth.

We were all in position with ten minutes to spare, and I sat at the balcony of the café with sweaty hands and a racing heart. I had an upside-down-mixed-up feeling about the whole operation. I was hoping Zara would walk through the door, partly because I was so curious about her and partly because I wanted to confront her about stealing the Trinity and Deckard plans. I wanted to know who Lazlo was. They didn't look at all alike. Maybe she was adopted or she was a runaway caught up in something awful. Maybe I could save her.

I had drifted into a sort of half sleep, not realizing how tired I was, all these questions running through my head. I should have taken Finn up on that cup of coffee; maybe then I'd have been more alert.

"Nothing yet," said Emily.

"Same," said Lewis.

"Bored," said Finn. "We need some action."

I shook my head and rubbed my eyes, trying to get myself fully awake. The café was getting a little rush of traffic so that I couldn't see Finn behind the line of four people. He couldn't see me, either, so he didn't notice when my jaw dropped at the sight of Zara's face on my screen. It was impossible. Me, with a standard Belinski just like Finn, and the tiny screen lit up with Zara's face.

"Hello, Adam," she said.

"I told you I'd be here," Zara said. "It's reassuring you actually showed up. Not so happy about all the friends you brought along."

"How are you doing this?" I whispered. I pressed the GPS function on the Belinski and toggled between two screens. Her location was blinking on Fifth Street, right where Finn's surveillance camera was pointing into a tree. She was within a hundred steps of where I sat.

Zara continued, "I'm going to ask you not to move from the balcony there, if that's all right with you. It's what Lazlo wants, and trust me, you don't want to cross him."

"Just keep him away from my friends," I told her.

The line of patrons was one person shorter and, to my horror, the seat where Finn should have been sitting was empty. In true Finn fashion he'd left the Belinski sitting on the table, half-hidden next to his backpack. I was about to ask Zara where Finn was, figuring by some form of additional trickery they'd taken him, when I realized what was really happening. Finn was standing at the cream and sugar station, pouring packets of sugar into his mouth.

"You asked me how I'm doing this," Zara said.

I jerked my head back to Zara, who was now staring up at me from what looked like the inside of a car.

"Seems like you left something in the water. Kudos to you for designing the watertight seal for the case."

I couldn't believe what she was telling me. "How did you get it?" I asked.

"Really, Adam," she said, "you should always have at least *one* person on your team who scuba dives."

"And I bet you scuba dive."

"For years."

Totally beautiful *and* she could deep-sea dive. Incredible.

You liked her, didn't you?

This girl had it all: a mysterious, pretty, code-slinging scuba diver. If it weren't for the fact that she was ruining my life, there's no doubt I would have followed her to the ends of the earth to get her attention.

"The real question is," she said, "how far are you willing to go in order to get your inventions back?"

"Well, what are we talking about here?" I asked.

Zara looked off to her left, distracted by something else, then she was back, whispering playfully this time.

"Sorry, I think you'll be hearing from Emily in just a second."

Emily piped in.

"Lazlo's on the move! Guys!" she said.

Zara laughed lightly, enjoying this game of cat and mouse. "Okay, well, maybe we could have coffee for real sometime," she said, then disconnected.

Finn was still guzzling sugar packets when Lazlo entered the café. It happened incredibly fast — he was there, then he was gone — I barely had a chance to see him at all. A few seconds after that, Finn sat back down and stared at the table as if he were made of stone. The Belinski was gone. He had been off his station for less than ninety seconds, but in that time, he'd managed to miss his assignment and let another camera slip into the hands of Lazlo and Zara.

"Get him!" I called.

Finn bolted out the door, looking both ways, trying to see where Lazlo had gone.

"Lazlo's got the Belinski," I told Emily and Lewis. "Either of you see him?"

"Looking," Emily said.

"Negative," Lewis said.

Finn looked back at me through the Grind House window and shrugged. It was clear Lazlo had gotten away.

I clicked in the GPS tracking for Finn's Belinski and watched the red dot bounce away from us. With his head start, there was no way we'd catch up.

I toggled to the GPS screen, reset to Lewis's Deckard. Nothing. She'd hacked into my hardware and disabled the GPS. No doubt she'd figured out a way to charge the Deckard whenever she wanted, too, so she could contact me at will. I toggled back to Finn's Belinski and saw that the red dot had stopped moving. Either Lazlo had frozen or he'd figured out he was being tracked and dropped the camera.

We were back to square one.

Zara was gone. She was toying with me, toying with all of us, but in a weird way I actually didn't mind.

I'd met my equal in this girl, and I aimed to win.

You fell for it — for her — that easily?

Yeah, I guess I did.

What about the others?

Finn felt so bad about losing the Belinski I didn't have the heart to give him a hard time.

"I messed it all up, didn't I?" he asked as soon I caught up to him.

"Nah, don't worry about it," I told him. "Besides, I think we can get the Belinski back."

"For real?" he asked.

"Yeah," I said. "For real. Follow me."

Finn and I walked toward the end of the block as Lewis came alongside and we all shared details of what had happened. Emily was nowhere in sight when my blinking GPS signal stopped us at a public garbage can and we peered inside. Finn's Belinski was perched on top of a half-eaten donut.

"Come to papa!" said Finn, fishing the camera out of the trash and holding it like a prized possession. While Finn wiped the screen on the Belinski, I asked Lewis if he'd seen anything from his vantage point on the cross street.

"Nothing. I heard Emily announce Lazlo's arrival, but that

was on the other end of the street. I just stayed where I was in case Zara showed up."

I nodded, glancing back toward the Grind House. There were probably twenty people on our side of the sidewalk, spread out along a hundred feet.

"Let's find Emily," I said. "Maybe she had better luck than we did."

When we rounded the corner at Fifth, we found Emily sitting down on the pavement, staring into her camera. We gathered around her, and when I tried to speak, she held up a hand.

"Hang on," she said. "I think I might have something here."

I wobbled back and forth, feeling the weight of thirty hours of sleeplessness catching up to me. If there had been a stiff wind, it would have blown me over for sure.

"Okay, I definitely have something," Emily said, standing up and putting the Trinity camera into her bag.

"What? You're holding out on us?" asked Finn. "Did you see him or not?"

Emily seemed to ignore Finn as she stared at me.

"You're not getting enough sleep," she said.

"Eww, you sound like his mom," said Finn.

"You want me to sound like your mom, too?" Emily challenged. "How 'bout if I say, 'Finn, you really need to focus more.' Or 'Finn, did you lose your camera again?' Or maybe 'Finn, can you explain to me why you got an F on this assignment?' "

"Ouch," Finn said.

"Okay, guys," I interrupted. "We get the point."

Emily made a face at Finn and we started walking back toward the Grind House, which was also in the direction of Henderson's Chip Shop.

"You're not going to believe who met me in the café," I said.

"Let me guess," said Lewis. "Bill Gates. He wants to hire you."

"Even weirder than that." I laughed, shaking my head. "Zara is also a scuba diver. She's the reason you didn't find your Deckard unit in the bay."

"No way," said Finn. "She's a programmer *and* a scuba diver? That's insane!"

Inside I was thinking, *Yeah, and you left out mysterious, beautiful, and dangerous.*

"She has my Deckard," said Lewis. Once in a while he got this very determined look on his face and his voice dropped an octave. It usually signified he was angry, which was a rare event.

"You guys, I got Lazlo going into the café," said Emily. "That part wasn't good for much, but when he left I was able to zoom in and get him before he got into a silver SUV."

We were back at the Grind House, and I started unlocking my scooter. Lewis was doing the same to his BMX, a look of determined calm on his face.

"I'm not sure," Emily continued, "but I think Trinity got something important when he got in the car. I need to get back to my station at home and do some slow-motion work."

"I've got something else I've been following up on," said Lewis. "I don't know if it's anything yet, but maybe."

It sounded like everyone but Finn had picked up a thread that might help us, so I jumped at the chance to head back to Henderson's. My brain was freezing up on me, shutting down after so much computing and concentrating. I was definitely running on empty.

"Okay, here's what we're going to do," I offered. "Emily, you and Lewis have leads to follow up on. Keep that going and load anything you've got into the interface as soon as you can. Finn, you get the footage of the Belinski and update the RMS. I'd like to see where the SUV was, Lazlo's path, everything. I'm going to grab a few hours of sleep, then I'll check in from the Vault."

Everyone agreed and we dispersed, heading in different directions. Finn would update the recon-map so we could start to piece together where we'd seen Lazlo and Zara so far. And all three of them would be working on footage from the stakeout. Hopefully, by the time I woke up, I'd be one step closer to catching Lazlo and Zara red-handed.

You can check out the interface here to account for everything that was uploaded while I slept. I even included the conversation I had with Zara on the Deckard.

It turns out I was even more exhausted than I realized. I slept right through the afternoon and the night, and didn't wake up until the next morning. A lot was uploaded while I slept, and it's all important to understanding what happened to us. Not only did Finn update the RMS, but there were two other videos uploaded as well.

Note: For a transcript of these videos, see Appendix G, page 174.

www.trackersinterface.com

PASSWORD

BELLEBOYD99

Surely, you must have been asking yourself why they had chosen you?

Well, it was obvious they'd been watching me. Not just when they put surveillance in the Vault, but *before* that. I know that hackers keep track of other hackers. And sometimes, I admit, when the Trackers found a hole in a system, we took credit. But why me? Was it because I was the best? Or was it because I was the most likely to fall into the trap? I couldn't figure it out. I thought it had to be one or the other. Really, it could have been both.

You were a victim of your own success.

Or maybe I just should have left the Glyphmaster alone when it came into my life. But, honestly, I wasn't thinking about any of that at the time. I just wanted to catch them, in the same way I'd wanted to crack the Glyphmaster. It was something I had to do. There was no reason to think about it too hard, because there was no getting out of it.

Having slept my way through an entire afternoon, evening, and night wasn't all bad. The Trackers had made some real progress, I felt completely revived and full of energy, and my dad's freeze on the use of the Vault had been lifted.

"Work on whatever you want, I'll take today's orders for the team," he said when I came into the shop. I knew this couldn't last. He'd come across a busted drive within a few hours and show up at the Vault door looking for help. But for now, his words were music to my ears.

Watching Lazlo's face appear in Finn's camera was startling enough, especially his menacing voice saying "Stop watching us." He knew we were tracking him and didn't like it one bit. But what was more startling was the slow-motion footage Emily had generated using the Trinity camera. She really knew how to dial in Trinity's best features, a lot of which had to do with how you shot the footage to begin with. It wasn't like shooting with an ordinary camera. You had to have a very steady hand and you needed the dexterity of a true gamer to hit the right buttons at the right time. In the right hands, Trinity was an amazing piece of technology. Watching Emily slow things down and sharpen the image of Lazlo walking to his car was pure genius. Such a small detail, but so important. At regular speed the envelope in the video was nothing more than a blur, but in the hands of a master with the right tools, evidence was there for the taking.

Blackfoot Holdings — two simple words on an envelope, words that might lead us closer to the answers we needed. As I watched the video once more, amazed by its crisp and fluid slowness, the Vault lit up with Finn's face.

"When you disappear, you *really* disappear," he said. "What happened?"

"Slept like the dead," I explained. This was something I figured he could relate to.

"You need to get a life, come skating with me sometime," Finn said.

"I think I need to get my life back first," I replied. "You know — from the people who stole it?"

Finn shrugged and said, "Yeah, I guess that's right. I checked out Emily's video — it's sweet."

I nodded my agreement and told him his wasn't too bad, either. It was our best look at Lazlo yet. "One thing is for sure," I said. "He and Zara don't seem to mind if we see them."

"Well," Finn said, "they have a pretty big hammer. You talk, they push a button, and everything you've ever worked on is public."

So that was the big threat?

Yes. You have to understand — hackers aren't polite people. They don't really care about annoying formalities like ownership or copyright. They only care about breaking into things — it's not like I could e-mail them all and say "Please give me my stuff back" if all of my work got out. Doesn't work that way. It would be like if someone stole Coca-Cola's secret formula and put it on the Web — anyone could brew it and there'd be no way for Mr. Coca-Cola to stop it. I'm not saying my inventions and my Tracker work was the same as that, but it was something. And there were a lot of people who'd offered me things for it over the years. If it got out, it was no longer mine. Simple as that.

Finn understood this. I think all of the Trackers did. And they knew it wasn't just my work that Lazlo had taken — it was everything we'd done as a group. Because the Vault had been our headquarters, our nervous system. Everything was stored there.

I think Finn saw how worried I was. "We'll find them," he said. "After all, tracking's what we do. It's in our blood."

I nodded.

"In the meantime," Finn went on, "can I come over there and see you? Some of the Belinski's guts are falling out."

I rolled my eyes. "Did you drop it?"

"Hey, no — I mean, maybe," he said. "It's just a little bit of a chip. And some tiny wires hanging outside the casing. Nothing serious."

It was hard to find anything that Finn took seriously, so *nothing serious* covered all the bases.

“Head on over,” I said, figuring it would take Finn at least half an hour the way he operated.

“I’ll be there in five,” he promised. “I’m right around the corner at the Grind House.”

I checked in as quickly as I could with Emily, and found she was making progress on Blackfoot Holdings. She was in research mode and just starting to get somewhere. I left her on the screen and watched her work in case anything big evolved, and then I went to work on my own projects. I watched Zara again, blowing the footage up to a larger size, and searched for anything that might give away something I didn’t already know. While I searched, it struck me that there was one noticeable omission in the Vault. No sign of Lewis.

I tried to hail him, but he didn’t pick up. He’d left a canned message on his Deckard that read I’M ONTO SOMETHING, OR MAYBE I’M NOT. I’LL CHECK BACK IN SOON.

This was a very Lewis thing to do, go totally off the grid for a while in pursuit of something. Best to leave him alone and let him come out when he was ready.

My dad appeared at the door of the Vault holding a laptop, with Finn trailing behind, riding his skateboard on the slick concrete floor of Henderson’s.

“Any chance I could get you to look at this one today?” my dad asked. “I think it’s a total bust, but I could be wrong.”

I looked at my watch.

“You only lasted twenty-seven minutes,” I told him.

My dad set the laptop on the corner of my desk with a sheepish look on his face. Then he said, “Oh, look, Finn is here. And he’s riding his skateboard in the shop even though I’ve told him at least a thousand times not to.”

“Sorry, Mr. Henderson. My bad,” said Finn, flipping his board expertly into the palm of his hand.

Dad made his exit before I could hand back the laptop and Finn sprung into the Vault, digging the Belinski out of his backpack. His eye caught the footage of Zara on one of the Vault screens.

"I can't believe she scuba dives," said Finn, shaking his head. "Probably has wicked ninja skills, too."

"Wouldn't surprise me," I said, and we both stared at the pretty face on the screen.

"Have you heard from Lewis?" I asked.

Finn shook his head. "Not since the surveillance mission yesterday. He's gone dark."

"Yeah, I noticed. That's good — it means he's into something big."

Finn handed me the Belinski, which didn't look to me like it had been dropped.

"Let's see what we have," I said, my mind taking on the roll of Mr. Fix-It once the device was in my hands. I turned the Belinski over and saw what Finn meant by guts falling out of the unit, but there was something all wrong about what I was seeing. Finn saw it on my face and reacted in typical fashion.

"Look, Adam, I'm telling you, I don't even remember dropping it. That stuff just showed up like a tick on a dog."

"Exactly," I said, grabbing a pair of industrial tweezers from the desk. "This little circuit and these two wires, they're not from inside the Belinski. Someone put them here."

"Whoa," said Finn, leaning in close for a better look.

"What are you two knuckleheads doing over there?" Emily piped in. She was staring down at us, watching with curiosity. "Hold that a little closer to your camera so I can see it better."

I tilted the Belinski to the side and rolled closer to one of the three Vault cameras so Emily could get a good look.

“You didn’t honestly think that came out of a Belinski?” she asked.

Finn was speechless. He’d picked up the camera from the garbage can and none of us had taken a close look at it. If we had, we’d have realized right away what had taken place.

“Lazlo put this here for us to find,” I said, popping the tiny circuit board off and spinning around in my chair. “That explains why he got rid of it so quickly.”

You’d been had.

Yeah, we’d been had.

21:11

I think we all knew we'd been tricked. I could see it on my friends' faces.

I leaned over to scrutinize the circuit board more, causing Emily to call, "Hey, come back!"

"Hold on," I told her. "I'm getting a better look."

Finn was leaning in so close I could feel him breathing on my shoulder. I held the chip and the two wires under a desk-mounted magnifying glass.

"You had the cinnamon roll at the Grind House, didn't you?" I said.

"*So* did! How'd you guess?" asked Finn, his voice way too close to my ear.

"Because you're, like, two inches from my face," I told him. "Do you mind?"

Finn edged away, but not by much, so I elbowed him in the arm.

"Backing off," he said quietly, as if we were carefully trying to dismantle a bomb and the slightest move might send us to the moon.

"You're not going to believe what's written on this chip," I said, more for Emily's benefit than Finn's. I backed away from the magnifying lens, shaking my head and almost laughing. I looked at Emily and almost couldn't bring myself to say the name.

"*Raymond*," I told her.

"You're kidding me," she said.

I shook my head no, and Emily looked as dumbstruck as I felt.

Who's Raymond?

That's what Finn said, totally confused. He wasn't the techno type like the rest of us, but still, Emily and I could hardly imagine the name hadn't come up with Finn around. We'd certainly talked about it.

"No, seriously, who's Raymond?" Finn asked again. "Don't leave me hangin'."

"It's not a who, it's a what," said Emily.

"You guys are punking me, right?" asked Finn. "Where's the camera?"

This struck me as a funny thing to say in a room *full* of cameras, and I could tell Emily felt the same way.

"This thing needs to be placed into a motherboard to activate," I told Emily. "You explain to Finn, and I'll crack open a piece of hardware."

I took the broken laptop my dad had left on the corner of the desk and deftly went to work while Emily gave Finn the rundown.

And what did she say?

"Raymond is a techno–urban legend, kind of like Shantorian —" she started.

"Hey, Shantorian is real, that's different," I interrupted.

"No one's ever seen him, so I doubt it," Emily persisted. "Anyway, Raymond is something no one's ever actually seen but everyone talks about. Apparently way back when the Internet first went public, this tiny group of powerful people built in a back door only they would ever know about."

"Cool," said Finn, for once listening with rapt attention as I ripped the back off of the laptop, exposing the motherboard.

Emily went on. "The legend claims that these few people — pioneers like Vint Cerf and Ted Nelson and Tim Berners-Lee —"

"Don't you mean Bill Gates and Steve Jobs?" asked Finn. "Who the heck are Vint, Ted, and Tim?"

I rolled my eyes and had to jump in on that one.

"Gates and Jobs are hardware and software," I explained, "but these Raymond legend guys, they're pure Internet. Vint Cerf invented TCP in 1974, which is still the backbone of the whole system. Ted Nelson invented Hypertext — you know what that is, right? It's all those links you click on when you're online. And Tim Berners-Lee — well, he basically created the World Wide Web. Any other questions?"

"I think that about covers it," said Finn. I could see he was starting to drift away, thinking about a trick he should be doing at the Green Lantern instead of listening to a geekfest.

"It might not have even been those three," Emily piped in. "I mean, there's so much secrecy with identities and pieces of early code, for all we know Raymond might have actually been a person."

"You guys are losing me," said Finn. "Booooooring."

"Well, maybe this will get your attention: Raymond is a door, okay? Imagine a way into the Internet that would let you see everything, no matter how secure you thought it might be. Bank accounts, government secrets, military data — *everything*. That's the legend. At the dawn of the Internet, sort of like the dawn of time I guess, someone created a secret door that could never be closed off."

"And only a few people have the key to that door, is that what you're telling me?" Finn asked.

"Not exactly," I said. I'd removed the motherboard from its casing and left the bad power supply behind, hooking it instead into my own Vault system. The board was a mess, but it worked.

"The Raymond code is what gets you in," I said.

So let me make sure we have this down right — Raymond was a back door to the Internet. Meaning?

Meaning that if you could get your hands on it, you'd have access to everything on the Web. And when I say everything, I mean *everything.*

Which could cause untold amounts of chaos?

Yes.

Even as Emily and I were telling Finn about it, I felt something stir inside me. *The Raymond code couldn't actually be real,* I thought. It was an elaborate joke — it had to be. But there was a tiny part of me that felt like I could be looking at something ominous and amazing. Ominous in the fact that if it was real, Raymond was incredibly dangerous. Amazing, because I could have in my possession the origins of the Web itself, and for a guy like me, that was an earth-shattering thought.

But why would Lazlo leave Raymond for you?

I had no idea. For all I knew, it was a big fake-out. But I needed to discover the truth.

I kept looking at the chip.

"It's got three light diodes: green, yellow, and red," I told Emily, spinning the small chip under the lens.

"You sound like a brain surgeon about to cut someone's head open," Finn observed.

I felt the same way, knowing how precious the chip could be, and I began thinking of how I might protect it, if it was in fact real. A plan was forming in my mind as I set the chip in place and attached one of the two wires.

"Are you sure you want that thing attached to the Vault when you hook it up?" Emily asked. "Remember what happened last time you had some equipment from Lazlo around."

"It's okay," I assured her. "We're just into one monitor and a power supply, nothing more. We should be fine."

"*Should* be fine?" asked Finn, sounding more dramatic as he went on. "That thing is radioactive tech. No doubt about it. What if it goes stealth on you — or worse, *Trojan*?"

Emily and I both stared at Finn as if he'd lost his marbles. He was trying to sound like an expert without having any idea what he was talking about. In situations like this it was always best to let Finn believe he was being useful. Trying to explain what was really going on would take way too long, and he'd go all glassy-eyed at the sound of tech jargon anyway.

Emily jumped in.

"I think Adam can handle this," she said, "but thanks for the warning. You never know when technology is going to go radioactive on you."

"Hey, no problem," said Finn, happy as a clam to have been helpful. "Just doing my part."

I attached the second wire and one of the nine Vault screens lit up. Emily couldn't see it and complained for a better view, so I positioned one of the Vault cameras directly in front of the monitor.

"Interesting," she said.

There were three old-school DOS prompts, really nothing more than green text on a black screen:

[1] READ ME FIRST
[2] THE THREE
[3] DO NOT IGNORE ME

"That last one sounds nice and friendly," said Finn. "You sure these guys weren't in the mob?"

I knew how to access the data the old-fashioned way, and within seconds I had accessed the Read Me First file. Green letters filled the screen.

Do you have a copy of the message?

Yes. One second.

At this point, the subject opened a file, then read the message aloud:

"This Read Me file is for you, Adam Henderson. You have the Raymond code now. You hold the key. I don't need to explain what it does, because you already know. The fact that you have it in your possession makes you a threat to national security. You, Adam Henderson, are a threat to every bank in the world. You're a threat to the United States military, the Pentagon, and the White House. To put it mildly, you are a dangerous young man. I can appreciate that.

"The time for turning back has passed.

"Zara"

And what was your reaction to this?

Well, Finn said, "This girl is *so* spooky — in a good way." And I wasn't about to argue.

Emily rolled her eyes, fully aware that at some level Finn and I had fallen under Zara's spell.

I activated The Three, overcome with curiosity about what it would reveal.

"Are you sure about this, Adam?" Emily asked, but there was no stopping me. Faced with this kind of information, I had no choice but to see what was behind each door.

Within The Three were folders:

[A] BANKS
[B] INTELLIGENCE
[C] THE RED BUTTON

"This looks bad," said Finn. "And what the heck is the Red Button? That sounds *really* bad."

I opened the Banks folder, which revealed dozens of files and scripts, all pointing to the fact that the Raymond disk was no joke.

How could you be sure?

There were security codes and information in those files that nobody — I mean nobody — could have gotten legally. They were from sites whose front doors were locked, bolted, and welded shut. So they only could have been obtained through a back door. I even went online and tried one of them out to be sure. Let me just say that within ten minutes, I was staring into accounts at the biggest bank in America. Raymond was the key.

I was standing at a gateway to trillions of dollars. I didn't have to look into the intelligence folder to know that it would be filled with the same kind of data, data that could lead the wrong person into the highest security areas of the Web. All of it — the bank accounts and the intelligence data — could be accessed secretly, through the one back door, and no one would ever be able to trace it.

"I can't believe it," said Emily. Her voice had turned shaky and scared, as if she were staring at a great monster about to eat us alive.

"You know what the Red Button does, don't you?" asked Finn. Even he was scared now. "What does it do?"

"They put it in there to account for a world gone mad with information," I said.

"Okaaay," said Finn, sounding more nervous than I'd ever heard him before.

"It shuts the whole thing down," said Emily.

He shook his head. "I don't get it."

"Finn," Emily said, "if the Red Button gets pushed, the Internet is over."

It was hard to get our minds around.

"That's like a joke, right?" Finn asked. "I mean, the banks and the intel, I can imagine that. But shutting the Internet down? That's gotta be impossible."

It *did* sound outrageous, but that was the legend. And what if it were true? I couldn't begin to imagine the total chaos the world would fall into if the Internet simply stopped working for even an hour. And the Raymond legend was much bigger than that.

"I've read all about this thing," I said, "but I still can't believe it's possible." I could hear the wonder in my own voice as I tried to imagine what this could mean. "Look, Finn, think of it this way: If you have ten blocks of wood piled on top of each other, the one at the bottom is the foundation, right?"

"Yeah," he said. "I can see that, sort of like Jenga. I'm unbeatable at that game."

"Okay, good — we have a visual. So the block on the very bottom, what's that one?"

"Like you said, that's the foundation. Everything else sits on top."

"Perfect!" I told him. "You're totally getting this."

Finn beamed.

I went on. "Okay, so now imagine if the bottom block of wood is hit from the side, really hard, with a hammer."

"That's easy," Finn said. "The whole thing is going down."

Right when the words left Finn's mouth the game was over. He got it.

"So the Raymond program is like a hammer," said Finn, the smile gone from his face. "It destroys the foundation."

"Couldn't have said it better myself," said Emily. "But I still think it's only a legend."

"Maybe that will tell us something," Finn said, touching the screen with his finger as he pointed to the only thing we hadn't looked at yet.

DO NOT IGNORE ME.

I clicked hesitantly on the link, half expecting orange smoke to roll out of the chip like poison gas.

"This oughta be good," said Finn, leaning in way too close over my shoulder again.

It was a note from Lazlo, and in the reading of it, our lives were turned upside down.

Here — this is what it said:

"We meet again. You're getting good at this, Mr. Henderson. As you can see, the Raymond program is real. Trust me on this. The Raymond legend is true. You now have in your possession the most powerful modern weapon known to man: the power to control information, open every door, take whatever you want. Only it's not quite so simple as that, as you shall soon see.

"So many codes, so little time.

"Zara tells me it shouldn't require more than ten hours for you to learn the Raymond scripts so that the routines can be run. You've no doubt looked at the folders, so you know what I'm talking about.

"I'm an easy man to please, if you stay focused on the task at hand. Ten hours — that is all I offer. If you miss the deadline, you will force my hand. And it won't just be your precious inventions and codes this time. You and your friends are in real danger, Adam."

He then listed each of our Social Security numbers, just to show he meant business — and that he could take our identities at any time.

"And Henderson's Chip Shop? Consider it bankrupt once I do some damage to your father's credit report and drain all the money out of his accounts.

"I realize you must be thinking, once again, about contacting the authorities, so I must be clear about the consequences. This is a life-or-death situation, Adam. I really hate to put things in such harsh terms, but there you have it.

"Let me be clear about one more thing: You think I am trackable. I assure you, I am anything but. I've never been found, and never will be. I can disappear faster than you can possibly imagine, and I see everything.

"Don't fail me, Adam Henderson.

"Lazlo."

You still had no idea what he wanted?

All that was clear at that point was that he wanted our silence. Or else.

Did you believe him when he said it was a matter of life or death?

I should've believed him more than I did.

How did your friends react?

Finn didn't waste any time responding to Lazlo's message.

"Is that my name and Social Security number in there?"

"All our names are in there," said Emily, as if she needed to. "He knows us all."

"Better not tell Lewis," Finn said. "He'll blow a gasket."

This was not the kind of pressure our buddy needed, but neither was it the kind of thing you didn't tell someone when you were in this deep.

"This Lazlo guy is about as serious as they come," I said. "Which is all the more reason we have to tell Lewis. He can't be involved unless he knows the risks."

"I'll make sure he knows," said Emily, an understanding in her voice that I hadn't ever heard there before. She, better than anyone, knew how to communicate with Lewis when things got crazy.

"Are you guys in?" I asked, not even sure if *I* was in. We could still call Lazlo's bluff. There was a good chance he and Zara would simply vanish, taking my work with them.

"Can you learn the Raymond program in time?" asked Emily.

"Please say yes," Finn pleaded, nervously spinning one of the translucent wheels on his skateboard.

I took a few seconds to reopen all the folders. I'd already been scanning with my eyes as we talked, but I wanted to make absolutely sure.

"It's a lot of coding," I said, "but ten hours is a long time. And I'm fresh off a good rest. I can already see some patterns here. I think I can do it."

"Good enough for me," Emily piped in. "I'm still working on something big over here, and I know Lewis is onto something, too. Let's all hunker down for a few hours and check back in if we find something."

"And tell Lewis," I reminded her.

Emily signed off, which left Finn loitering in the Vault trying to figure out what he should do. The rest of us had something to focus on, but Finn was in perpetual motion.

"I'm thinking you need to blow off some steam," I said. "Give me three or four hours here; you go hit the Green Lantern and nail that move you've been working on."

Finn's face lit up.

"The Monster Roll," he said, awestruck. "A thing of beauty if ever there was one."

Finn started to explain in language that was as foreign to me as programming was to him. I let him go on, walking him to the front door of Henderson's as he got more and more excited. It was a long trick, consisting of at least five moves from different sides of the ramp. I heard the term *three-sixty* more than once, and an indecipherable list of words like *pivot*, *fakie*, and *grab*.

"Dude, are you sure this is okay?" he asked before he left. "I mean, you guys are all working and stuff. Is this really the best use of my time?"

He was looking at me like he sometimes did, when he felt a sense of uselessness among a pack of geeks.

"We need the real Finn more than ever," I assured him. "Before we know it I have a feeling we're going to be tracking again, and everyone will be stressed out. You keep us light on our feet, mellow out all the serious stuff. Best thing you can do right now is stay loose and wait for a call."

Finn was so excited he dropped his board on the sidewalk and performed a kick flip, something I couldn't dream of doing. He made it look easy, but I knew it was anything but.

"Thanks, Adam," he said. "I won't let you down. The Monster Roll is mine."

Finn rolled away, happy as a clam, and I wished my biggest concern was landing a complicated skateboarding move.

22:10

So you plunged right in?

No, I played some video games and went to a movie. Are you kidding me? I had a grand total of ten hours to unlock the most important technology in the world. Of course I plunged right in! What else was I going to do?

Okay, I get it. What I meant was: You didn't hesitate, not even a little? You didn't worry about what you were about to do? You didn't think to yourself, *Maybe this is illegal. Maybe I'll end up behind bars. Someone might get hurt, even killed.*

As far as I was concerned, cracking the Raymond code didn't do any harm. It wasn't the code itself that was the problem — it was what someone might do with it. Since I knew I wasn't about to cause chaos, I felt it was safe in my hands. In fact, there was a part of me that felt it was my duty to crack that thing open. If I could do it I'd be in control. Better me than Lazlo, I can tell you that much.

Within about three hours, I was churning through code at record speed. This was very common for me, and something I never really talked about with anyone. It was one of my carefully guarded secrets, and it was coming in handy right about then. When it came to programming, my mind worked like a snowball rolling down a hill. I started slow, but once I began getting the hang of what I needed to do, I went faster and faster, until my hands couldn't keep up with the lines of code firing in my head.

I was pretty sure Lazlo wouldn't have accounted for my

ability to race through the work I needed to do in order to unlock the banks, the intel, and the Red Button, but I could tell I was only a few of hours from unlocking it all. This would leave me time to do two things I knew I had to accomplish: build a safer housing for the Raymond chip and create a Raymond firewall. I was determined to lock things down tight so only I could gain access to what lay behind an unlocked Internet.

My Belinski started playing theme music from the old *Batman and Robin* show, and I knew instantly who was trying to reach me.

Zara.

She still had Lewis's Deckard camera, the one she'd used to contact me in the Grind House. I picked up the Belinski and answered the call, flipping the miniature video monitor on.

"I was wondering if you'd ever call me again," I said. "I see you're still using my equipment. I hope it's treating you well."

I couldn't tell where Zara was. Definitely not indoors, but for all I knew, she was in another state by now.

"It's a beautiful day outside, in case you wanted to know," Zara told me. "I know how it can be, staring into a screen all the time. Pretty soon it's night and a whole day has disappeared unseen."

I didn't care about Zara's philosophical musings. I wanted answers.

"Why don't you just run away from Lazlo?" I asked. "We could protect you."

"*You* protect *me*?" she scoffed. "From *Lazlo*? Really, Adam, you need to be more realistic."

"Next you're going to tell me you have killer ninja skills."

Zara looked at me as if to say *You expected anything less?*

"What planet are you from?" I asked, completely blown away all over again. "No, don't even answer that, just tell me why you're doing this. Stealing my work — okay, that's not cool, but it's also not dangerous — but now my friends are in real trouble. This Lazlo guy, he's not messing around. Why would you get involved with someone like that?"

Zara wasn't going to give me an inch. "Yours is not to ask why, Adam," she said. "Yours is to program. Isn't that the most important thing?"

"And what if I don't? What if I call the police right now? Do you actually believe he'll resort to violence? I don't think so."

I was calling their bluff, hoping to get Zara to rethink her actions. But I should have known better. A few seconds later Lazlo's face was in the screen, the same infuriating smirk plastered across his face.

"I believe Zara asked you a question. I'd like an answer. Oh, and before I forget, I wanted you to know Lewis and Emily are both still in their rooms, and Finn is still skating at the Green Lantern. That's just in case you're looking for them. Or, I suppose, if I need to find them."

He really could see everything. Lazlo was able to get to my friends any time he wanted, and quickly, it seemed. What if he could somehow tell if I called 911? What if he was secretly tapped into my all my online accounts? If I put the word out by phone or by computer, chances were he'd know faster than I could blow my nose.

You were trapped.

Yes. I was trapped.

Lazlo looked at his watch. "Your time is almost half gone."

"Progress is slow," I lied. "I'm going to need every second of the ten hours."

"That will be fine," Lazlo replied. "When you finish, place the chip inside a white envelope. Drop the envelope into the same garbage receptacle where I left your camera earlier. I'll take it from there." He handed the Deckard back to Zara.

"I better let you get back to work," Zara said. "I wouldn't want to be a distraction and have you finish five minutes late. What a tragedy that would be."

"Wait —" but it was too late. Zara signed off. I had a picture in my mind of her doing a series of sweet karate moves on Lazlo, then riding a Harley over to Henderson's to tell me she'd seen the error of her ways.

But of course, ninja skills or not, that kind of scene was not in the cards. I was about to go back to programming when the Vault lit up. Emily and Lewis were calling in at the same time, and I was about to get some much-needed good news.

The interface is loaded with new information, all of it critical to understanding where things went from here. I can keep going. I'm not tired. We're coming to a big part and I'm raring to go. But it's all going to fit together like a puzzle if you'll hear my side of the story exactly as it went down.

Here's what you'll find:

- A video from Lewis, revealing something big
- A video from Emily, revealing something even bigger
- A totally unexpected video from Lazlo
- An updated RMS

Check it out:

Note: A transcript of these videos can be found in Appendix H, page 180.

www.trackersinterface.com

PASSWORD

SASUKESARUTOBI

22:29

You see — now we were cooking with fire! Not only had Lewis pulled off the techno-magic trick of a lifetime, Emily had also found something worthy of investigation.

I'd always known this day would come, and I was thrilled beyond words at the information Lewis and Emily had discovered. If you can imagine inventing the paintbrush, then putting it in Michelangelo's hand, you'll get a sense of how I felt at that moment. It was one thing to invent a brand-new device, but what was truly amazing was watching a master *use* that device. Emily was showing great promise with the Trinity, and Lewis had clearly become a master of the Deckard while I wasn't paying attention.

"So what do you think?" Lewis asked me after showing me what he'd done. So nonchalant, but with a hint of *Yeah, I did that. Amazing, huh?*

"Lewis, you've painted a masterpiece," I said. "I'm in awe."

"Me too," said Emily, not the least bit jealous that her discovery, although very useful, wasn't nearly as compelling as Lewis's.

He had managed to find the location of Lazlo's hotel room in a clever and sophisticated way, using the Deckard and his own tools to take my work to a whole new level. Seeing the church steeple in the background of Zara's videos was just the start. Finding it, now that was a trick of epic proportions. It was one of the coolest videos I'd ever seen, period.

"Once I found the church, it was really just a matter of simple math," said Lewis.

"Simple math? I don't think so," I said. Not only had Lewis discovered the church steeple, he'd used the Deckard to zoom to the right level, swung the view around, and found the only hotel that could have been the one — absolutely amazing. If I hadn't seen the video I wouldn't have believed it myself.

"And you, Emily, your slow-motion capture of the folder is huge. Way to go," I said, trying to spread the praise around.

"It was just a matter of staying on him, then going through everything I had one frame at a time," she explained. "We got lucky, because obviously Blackfoot Holdings is how they're planning to launder the money if you open the banks for them. You're not doing that, are you?"

"I've got it covered, don't worry," I answered.

The pieces were starting to fall together. Emily had slowed Lazlo down, catching a glimpse of a folder sticking out of his attaché case. The tab on the folder read BLACKFOOT HOLDINGS, but at regular speed, no way anyone could have caught that. Emily had to really dig to get this important piece of evidence.

"The Web site doesn't have much, just the video and a logo to make it look legit," Emily raced on. "They're obviously planning to have you open the banks with the Raymond, then pass the money through Blackfoot. They have branches all over the world, Adam. At least twelve — that much I've figured out. They're not in the news, very secretive, only 'qualified investors,' which I'm guessing is no one at all."

"They must be using us so the back door can't be traced to them," said Lewis. "We're going to be in some serious trouble if we do this."

I glanced at Emily, looking for whether or not she'd told Lewis about Lazlo's directives.

"She told me," Lewis said, "so you don't have to worry. I'm not going to let this guy win."

"Lewis," I said, "you are a prince."

He just shrugged. "Nope, just a guy with a camera."

“And modest — I love that in a man,” said Emily. She was joking, of course, but it was clear she was impressed.

“Okay, so we know where the hotel is and we know about Blackfoot,” I said. “We’re two steps ahead of them, three if I can get this programming done.”

“How’s that going?” asked Lewis.

“Pretty good. I need, like, two more hours. I’ve got a plan I think might help us. Can you guys find Finn and meet me in, say, two and a half hours?”

“No problem,” said Emily. “I can ride by the Green Lantern and shake him loose.”

“Just be careful,” I said. “Somehow, Lazlo has your location. You’ll have to find a way to lose him.”

“Can do,” Lewis said, although I detected a little shake in his voice. “Where do we meet?”

“In the parking lot of the Windsor Hotel, where else?” I said. “Get ready for the biggest test of your lives. And prepare to meet Orville.”

“For real?” they both asked at once.

I nodded. This was no time to hold back.

Orville was about to get its first test . . . and the stakes couldn’t have been higher.

It took every second of the two hours I'd allotted myself to finish the work I needed to complete. The banks and the intel were open, creating one of the strangest experiences of my life as I sat in the Vault. It was like standing at the edge of the Grand Canyon, looking at the vast opening and wondering . . . how did this even get here? Seeing the opening I'd just created made me realize how infinite the Internet was, and more important, how much money changed hands with the click of a mouse. I wasn't looking at billions of dollars in transactions. I was looking at trillions upon trillions. I could see that it would be possible for Lazlo to essentially reach in and grab whatever he wanted. It had the makings of the biggest robbery in the history of the world. In fact, every robbery before it could be added together and it wouldn't be this big.

Weren't you tempted?

What?

All of that money, right there. With a few clicks you could have guaranteed your family's fortunes for the rest of your life. No one would have known. I'm sure you could've covered your tracks. You had to be tempted.

Look, of course I was. I won't lie.

So what stopped you?

I wouldn't have been able to live with myself.

Really? That's going to be your story?

It's true.

You had trillions of dollars at your fingertips, and you were worried about living with yourself?

That, and I didn't want Lazlo to win.

I see.

I'm not sure you do. Maybe in the same situation you'd steal everything.

It's you we're talking about here, not me. But considering what happened next, it's strange you showed such restraint. That's what I'm saying. Now continue your story. You were looking into the Grand Canyon. Then what?

My dad interrupted me. He knocked, entered, and spoke all in one fluid motion and I nearly jumped out of my chair.

"All rested up and ready for more?" he asked.

The last thing I needed was my dad looking over my shoulder getting all curious, so I switched my screen to a testing sequence.

He shot me a questioning glance.

"I'm creating a program for these new drives that keep coming in," I explained. "They're getting bigger — the drives I mean — and it's taking too long. We should probably start charging more."

"Hmmm," my dad said, glancing at my screen. "You might be right. Either way, I've got orders on the counter. Can I drop a couple at your door?"

"Yeah, sure, but I'd like to finish this first if I can," I told him. "Then I've got some plans tonight with the gang, something I can't get out of. Can I do them in the morning or late tonight?"

My dad rubbed his chin and twisted his face with a look that said, *Dude, you're really putting me out here.*

"I suppose, if you have to," he said.

My dad left the room without shutting the door. I waited a few seconds, then kicked it closed. I know what you're going to say — if only I'd told him everything right then, it would've all been different. But I was already too deep into it, you see that, right? And what I was doing was so big, so dangerous, that I couldn't trust anyone else.

Not even my own father.

I switched my screen back to the Raymond program. Then I toggled away from the entry point I'd just discovered for the world banking system, and I could literally feel my blood pressure spiking. There was something about staring into an endless sea of classified CIA folders, all of them one click away from being accessed, that made me feel light-headed. It was a real face melter, let me tell you. In a matter of seconds I could become the most notorious spy the world had ever known. I could send intel all over the planet, swapping secrets, simply by grabbing and releasing. Or worse, I could take secrets from all the biggest governments and simply dump them online for everyone to see. Needless to say, I had no interest in opening even one classified folder, and I sure didn't want someone like Lazlo having access to this kind of power. It was a disaster waiting to happen.

And the Red Button?

The Red Button was another matter entirely. That thing was off the charts complicated. It wasn't the sort of thing that could be solved in twenty hours, let alone ten, given everything else I had to do. And the Red Button was locked down with a monstrous level of complexity, which was appropriate, given the fact that if I did crack the code I'd be one click away from disabling the World Wide Web. The thought of it alone was beyond outrageous.

So there I was, staring at a world of problems I'd been forced to unlock, with a few hours left before Lazlo would expect me to deliver. Any real programmer would know the Red Button was not something that could be done this fast, and Zara was clearly on my level in the brains department. No, they didn't care about that part. The Red Button wasn't in their game plan, and I had a feeling the intel wasn't, either. They wanted the banks, the money — that was their entire game. I felt sure of it. That's why they'd put it on the top of their list.

"Time for a firewall," I said, opening a folder on one of the drives I hadn't touched in over a year. Before I could click on it, Emily's screen lit up.

"Adam, you there?" she asked. "I've got Finn and Lewis in the room."

Emily checked her watch as Finn and Lewis leaned in closer so I could see them.

Emily went on, "You said to leave you alone until you were down to exactly two hours so you could concentrate."

"Time's up," said Finn. "How'd it go?"

Lewis looked like he was waiting for bad news.

"Lewis, you okay with all this?" I asked, sure he was feeling in way over his head.

He surprised me with the quickness of his answer.

"If there's any chance we can stop them, we have to try," he said. "I'm ready to roll."

I felt a wave of optimism and smiled for the first time in I couldn't remember how long.

"I'm on schedule with the Raymond disk," I told them. "We're in good shape there. But I'm going to need a little longer to make sure they never get their hands into those bank vaults."

"What about the intel and the Red Button?" asked Emily.

"Got that covered, too," I assured her. "What I need is for you guys to do some serious tracking while I wrap this up. So here's the plan."

"This oughta be good," said Finn, a wide, toothy grin spilling across his face.

I let Emily run through what they'd discovered about

Blackfoot Holdings, which was exactly as I'd expected. It was an international front, nothing more, but behind the façade there were clues to their plans.

"As best I can tell, they're going to move the money into thousands of micro-accounts all over the globe so it's harder to trace," Emily said.

Lewis jumped in: "It looks like they might transfer the money several times, confusing the system as they go. And I'd bet they're looking to take at least a billion, maybe more."

"It sounds like a lot," said Emily, "but in the scheme of things, it's a tiny number. I think they plan to move trillions, but let most of it leak back in. By the time everything is sorted out, the missing billion will be long gone, sifted through thousands of different accounts on every continent."

"This is crazier than crazy," said Finn. "Who comes up with this stuff?"

"Everyone listen carefully," I said. "I have to stay on the work here, but your job is going to be just as important. Here's what you're going to do."

I explained the mission in detail over the next ten minutes. They had to figure out what room Lazlo and Zara were using, get inside, and place surveillance cameras. If the Trackers could pull it off, then we could do our own recording of everything. I'd have the evidence I needed to stop Lazlo and Zara.

"Adam, what about all your work?" asked Emily.

"I think we're way past worrying about what happens to our stuff," I said.

The situation had gone beyond thinking about gadgets and code. If all I cared about was getting my stuff back, I was no better than Lazlo and Zara.

Finn piped in: "If we turn them in, they'll post everything.

Before you know it they'll be selling my Belinski at Walmart for ninety-nine bucks."

"The Deckard would go for at least two hundred," said Lewis. I could already see these guys imagining the Trackers devices lining the shelves in shiny boxes.

"Let's stay focused on what we need to do," I said, steering us back into thinking like a team. "Emily, can you get over here fast? I need to give you a new piece of equipment you're going to need."

"The Orville," said Lewis. "Based on the name, I can only guess what you've cooked up in the Vault."

"I'll be there in ten," said Emily.

"Perfect," I said. "Finn, you and Lewis know what do to."

"Windsor Hotel, here we come," Finn replied, looking relaxed after a few hours of skating at the Green Lantern.

At any point, did you tell them the power you had?

Sure. I mean, they knew what was at stake.

But right then — you didn't tell them that you could already access all the banks, did you? You kept it to yourself.

Yeah. Why?

It's just an interesting secret to have kept.

There was no need for them to know.

You mean, there was no need for you to share.

I really appreciate how you keep putting words in my mouth. Next you'll be telling me I have a billion dollars stashed somewhere.

Do you?

No!

Look, I wasn't even thinking about taking someone else's money. Not then, not *ever.* We had an hour and a half left. I switched gears, totally focused on the work I had to get done before Lazlo and Zara contacted me again. I went back to the folder I'd opened before the Trackers made contact, and started digging for just the right collection of icons. Zara didn't know it, but she wasn't the only one who had made Glyph images that weren't part of the project. I had made well over a hundred images for words that were too obscure for a one hundred fifty word language. I'd picked all my favorite words and made Glyph symbols out of them for practice. Plus I loved making Glyphs, so for a while it was an obsession I couldn't get enough of.

By the time Emily showed up at the door to the Vault, I'd already created a firewall puzzle for the banks entryway. When Lazlo clicked into the banks expecting to see an open door, he was going to encounter a Glyph puzzle only I could solve.

"Nine minutes," Emily said, a little out of breath but satisfied that she'd reached me faster than promised. I spun in my chair and unlocked a file drawer, then took out the Orville so Emily could see it.

"Wow, that's a big controller," she said. "Must be complicated."

"Not really," I told her. "I needed a big housing so I could create some new signaling. The Orville can fly ten miles away and I can still control it."

Emily shook her head and said, "No way."

"Yes way," I said. "I've already tested it."

Emily closed the door behind her and came up beside me for a closer look.

"*So* cool," she said.

The Orville was a flying camera of the highest order. A smaller version of the Wi-Fi Belinski was mounted to a double-blade helicopter, and the remote control saw everything Orville saw.

"Wherever he flies, I can see what Orville sees," I said.

"Adam, this is incredible," Emily told me. "And I know just how you plan to use it."

She'd already put two and two together. If we could fly up the side of the Windsor Hotel, we could peer inside each room until we found the one we were looking for.

"I'm not flying it," I said. "You are."

Emily's face lit up. She was our best remote control expert, amazing with hot rods.

"I figure it can't be that big a leap from driving a remote control monster truck to flying a remote control helicopter," I said.

"I've flown gliders and planes," she said, reaching out for the controller and messing with the joysticks. "This won't be a problem."

The Orville whirled to life and Emily expertly flew it around the Vault, watching the screen as it showed everything in its path.

I glanced at my watch. There was only an hour to go.

"You better get into action," I told her. "I'll be watching from here once the mission launches. Let's shoot for twenty minutes from right now."

"We'll be ready," Emily promised. "I think I'm in love," she added as I opened the door, completely comfortable that Emily could handle the new device. As she walked out the door, Orville leading, the camera caught my dad coming toward us. Emily lifted Orville near the ceiling, said hello to my dad, and kept right on going, leaving the Orville safely outside for me to pick up once Dad was gone.

"What the heck was that all about?" Dad asked.

"A little something I've been working on in my spare time," I answered, hoping this would be a very brief father-son encounter.

He nodded appreciatively. This was probably the hundredth time something new had come out of the Vault. Just because this invention was flying didn't mean it was going to surprise my dad.

"Dropped three orders outside your door," he said. "I'll pick 'em up in the morning, okay?"

"No problem," I said. "I've just gotta stay on this coding and get it ready. You're going to like it."

"I'm sure I will," he said.

I practically pushed him out of the Vault. Lazlo expected the unlocked Raymond chip in less than an hour, and I still had to lock down the intel section. There was also the matter of creating a safe housing for the chip, something I'd been thinking about for hours and already had figured out in my head.

I knew if I didn't protect the Web, it would be entirely vulnerable.

And that, to put it mildly, stressed me out.

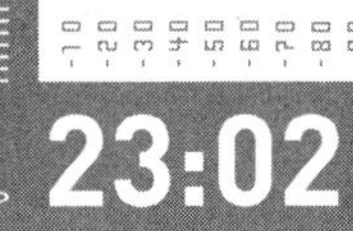

I finished a new Glyph puzzle for the intel portion of code and locked it down. In theory, the setup would be perfect. It would appear as though I'd unlocked everything and created the openings Lazlo and Zara expected. There were several prompts along the way, all of which would work as expected, but the final click would reveal the Glyph wall, where the whole operation would screech to a halt.

Or so I hoped. There was no time to test it.

I removed the chip from the motherboard I'd attached it to and went straight to work on the housing. I'd chosen a certain flash drive casing with a USB port and light diodes to match my needs. A few soldering points, three tiny screws, and the chip was safely hidden. Now, if it got dropped or even stepped on, the Raymond chip was likely to survive.

There were three lights hidden under a twist cap on one end: green, yellow, and red. Green and yellow were lit up to indicate Banks (green) and Intel (yellow) were live. The red light was not lit, indicating the Red Button had not been activated. Grabbing a red Sharpie, I marked the front of the black casing with a letter *R* and breathed a sigh of relief. The trap was set. I typed out a hurried message describing the setup for Lazlo, printed it out, and dropped the Raymond disk and the note into an envelope.

With twelve minutes to spare, I raced out of the Vault and through Henderson's, boarding the Roadrunner to go to the Grind House. The drop went down without incident as I rode past the garbage can where we'd found the Deckard the day before. I dropped the Raymond disk without stopping, jumped the curb, and headed back to the Vault as fast as my scooter would carry me.

On the short ride back to the chip shop I thought about one thing in particular: The time had come to bring down Lazlo and Zara. They'd hacked into my system, stolen everything I'd ever worked for, and messed with my friends. I was as determined as I'd ever been in my life, and everything was about to come to a head.

After launching the Orville, I returned to the Vault, ready to monitor as my friends infiltrated Lazlo and Zara's hotel.

But, as you'll see, it ended up being much harder than that.

If ever there was a time when looking at the mounting evidence mattered, this is it. I've uploaded a new video into the interface, and basically, it blows this thing wide open.

Please stop taping me. I see you behind those mirrors. Stop watching me!

Step away from all those devices and see with your own eyes what happened to me and my friends.

A transcript of this video appears in Appendix I, page 184.

www.trackersinterface.com

PASSWORD

MARTINCOOPER

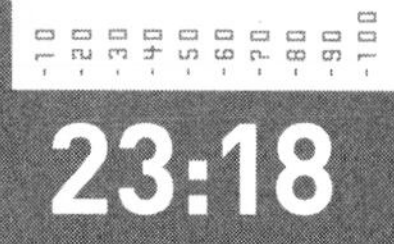

How do I explain what it felt like to watch and experience everything that happened in that video? It was, in order of appearance, satisfying, exciting, and scary.

Satisfying because the Orville performed a miracle in a real-life situation, flying up the side of the Windsor Hotel and seeing Zara's statue sitting on the windowsill. Watching my own invention perform so admirably made me feel like all my work had really meant something. The events of that night were exciting, too, because we reached a whole new level as a team of Trackers: finding the right room, creating diversions, making swipe cards, entering rooms, and most important, placing surveillance cameras in locations I didn't think were possible.

Then everything changed.

You got that right. The whole situation turned terrifying in a way that I wasn't prepared for. All the way up until Lazlo and Zara arrived in the room, there was still a part of me that imagined the whole thing as a game we were playing. No one had gotten hurt. There had been threats, sure, but they hadn't seemed real. That all changed when Finn and Lewis were trapped in the upper reaches of a towering hotel, within a few feet of a guy who really did seem like he might harm them. It was the first time I thought I might lose them forever, and it scared the living daylights out of me.

You see now why you should have come to me sooner.

You don't know the whole story. Not yet. And besides, I never came to you. It was the other way around.

Nonetheless, you put your friends in real danger. What if they'd never come out of that room alive. Then what?

But that's not what happened. I mean, I admit it now — I should have called someone or at least told my dad — but we were in so deep. We weren't thinking clearly.

That appears obvious. Maybe it was the money that blinded you. Maybe that's why your friends didn't come out of this like you thought they would.

I told you I didn't take anything. Why won't you believe me?

Because the evidence doesn't add up.

You want evidence? I'll give you evidence. You think this is over. You think you've seen something. But I'm just getting started.

Do tell.

I don't like you.

I'm not interested in whether you like me or not, Adam. I'm interested in what you did to your friends. That and what you're not telling me about Raymond.

Wanna see another video?

I don't know, do I?

Oh, I think you do. I think you're ready to have your mind blown, just like mine was.

Show me.

Subject went to work on the keyboard. His hands were flying, pages opening, items being moved from place to place. He was clearly hiding something.

There. Now you can see the lies and the truth all in one place. Have a ball.

Subject pushed computer toward me, turned away, revealed new password.

Note: A transcript of this video is presented in Appendix J, page 196.

www.trackersinterface.com

PASSWORD

LAZLOSPEAKS

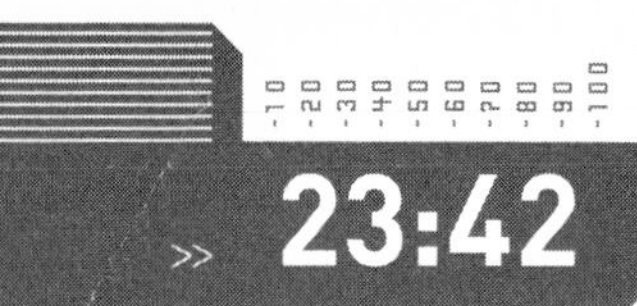

Well, that was a surprise. But it doesn't change anything.

What do you mean it doesn't change anything? It changes *everything*! They lied to us.

And you find this hard to believe, coming from two people who tricked you into activating the Raymond program?

It's almost midnight. When do we stop?

When I say we stop.

Are my friends okay?

You tell me. No — I take that back — tell me how you felt after you found out the entire thing was a setup. Then we'll talk about your friends.

The reality of what was happening to us hit me like a piano falling from a building. I felt stupid, which I suppose is very satisfying for you. But I'm not a dumb guy, at least I don't think I am. Still, there's no getting around it: We were royally duped from start to finish.

I told you.

I'll never forget when Zara said those words to Lazlo.

I thought the same thing everyone else did. We'd caught them on tape, trying to hack into banks. We'd double-crossed them and won. But I was wrong, probably more wrong than I've ever been in my life.

My inventions weren't at risk of being stolen.

My life and the lives of my friends weren't in danger.

Lazlo and Zara were not thieves of the highest order.

No, not one of those things turned out to be true.

I'd been beaten at my own game, pushed to the breaking point, never considering the fact that the whole thing might be a setup. From the very start, it was all an elaborate test, one with a different kind of consequence than I had envisioned.

Not only were my inventions not in jeopardy of being leaked onto the Net for anyone to take, Lazlo and Zara claimed they wanted to use them for work that really mattered. Real situations battling the biggest online criminal of them all: Shantorian. The name alone made the hair stand up on the back of my neck. In the blink of an eye the renowned hacker turned into my chief enemy, and my best work could be used to draw him out and hunt him down. The thought of it was exciting beyond anything I'd done before.

ISD, the Internet Security Directive, that's what they called it. Lazlo said he ran the secret operation, and Zara was his first recruit. Top secret, government funded, and extremely exclusive, he said ISD needed something more than the brilliant programmer it had found in Zara. It needed young, street-smart trackers to achieve its all-important purpose: to bring down Shantorian. Lazlo and Zara were anything but thieves; they were on the cutting edge of technology, putting everything they had into capturing the most dangerous criminal mastermind on the planet.

How could I say no? How could *any* of us say no? This was a chance to use our skills and equipment for something that really mattered. I won't lie, the thought of using my inventions for such a daring and important cause was beyond awesome. The data alone would validate what I already knew: My equipment rocked.

And my team? They were the best group of trackers anywhere.

So you joined forces with ISD, an agency so secretive even I've never heard of them.

Lazlo wasn't about to make it that easy. We weren't going to step right in and run the place. Sure, we'd proved ourselves, but not enough. Not *nearly* enough.

I don't understand.

We had to prove ourselves one more time.

A test?

Yeah, a test. But nothing like the ones we'd done on our own. This test made me realize something I hadn't been completely sure of before: Whatever ISD was, the guy running it was willing to put our lives at risk in order to get what he wanted.

How did the rest of the Trackers react to the idea of joining ISD?

I remember Lewis saying, "This sort of puts Zara in a whole new light, you think?" I was sitting in the Vault, my dad completely unaware of what was about to happen across town, and Lewis was talking to me from a remote location, sitting on his bike.

"Yeah, she's still mysterious," Finn said, also waiting at a secret location. "And hotter than hot."

"You do realize I can hear you?" said Zara. I don't know *where* she was.

Finn didn't respond. Zara's silky voice had turned him mute where he stood on his skateboard.

"I'm going to be completely honest with you, Zara," Emily said. She was in position, ready to roll, staring into the Trinity camera. "I'm still not sure I trust you."

"Fair enough," Zara said. "But you can. I promise."

"Let's stay focused on the mission, guys." It was my job to make sure everything ran smoothly, and I didn't want to blow it. I knew Emily could be combative and I needed her full attention on the dark hallway where she stood. "Nothing matters if we don't pass this test."

"I'm ready," Lewis said.

"Ready to roll," Finn agreed, grinning from ear to ear at the thought of charging into high gear.

Emily had a look on her face in the shadows that made her feelings clear: *I was born ready.*

So you could see everyone from your location?

Yeah, the Trackers were all in place.

But you weren't out there with them, were you? You stayed in the safety of the Vault while your friends were in real danger.

No, that's not the way it happened. I was their leader. It was my job to watch, to relay instructions. I could only do that from the Vault.

Whatever you say. The fact is you were safe, they were at risk. They might not have lived to tell what they knew.

What are you implying? That I wanted them to fail? Or something worse?

Fill in the blanks, Adam. The evidence is hard to deny.

When am I going to see my friends?

That depends. Which one do you want to see?

All of them, of course!

That might prove difficult.

What do you mean? What did you do with them?

I could ask you the same thing, Adam. Just show me the video. Then we'll talk about who you will and won't see.

Fine.

Note: A transcript of this video appears in Appendix K, page 202.

www.trackersinterface.com

PASSWORD

SHANTORIAN

You're right about one thing. Lazlo is more than willing to risk the lives of his followers.

You make him sound like the leader of a cult. That's not it at all. Lazlo ran ISD and we helped him.

If you'd known how this was all going to turn out, would you have still tried to join ISD?

All I can say is we were Trackers. It's what we did. We were recruited into a top secret organization to do real work bringing down real criminals. We'd gone from being kids with gadgets to undercover agents working for the highest level of government.

It's midnight and we have a long way to go. What happened next, after the test? What did you do as a member of ISD? Where is the Raymond program?

I've shared everything I'm comfortable sharing. I've told you all the facts that led me and my friends into ISD. If you want the rest of my story, you're going to have to play by my rules. I've got one demand before I show you anything else.

What might that be, Adam?

Bring me Finn or this interview is over.

Postscript to interview session number 1 with Adam Henderson.

We continue our investigation into ISD. Mr. Henderson claims this organization is covert, and therefore unknowable to someone like me. I find this increasingly hard to believe and remain convinced of Mr. Henderson's guilt. He has concocted a world within a world to hide his true intent, but there is still the matter of the missing billions, and all roads lead to the Trackers. They're hiding something. All of them are.

Adam Henderson sleeps. I'll give him an hour, no more.

Then the gloves come off.

Insp. Ganz, close file 1, 00:35.

» APPENDIX A

The following is a transcript of the video shown by Adam Henderson at 17:38 to H. Ganz in Room 214. Transcription and analysis by H. Ganz.

A marker, ***OPEN VFILE 2630****, indicates some kind of media asset filing system. Below this identifier it reads:* ***PROPERTY OF ADAM HENDERSON | DO NOT COPY OR DISTRIBUTE***

An image appears of four young people, seen from behind, apparently on a rooftop at sunrise or sunset, three males and one female. A voice, apparently that of suspect Adam Henderson, is heard:

Adam (voice-over)

We did missions. Field exercises. Sometimes it was more like equipment testing.

The image changes to a new one, in black-and-white, of what appears to be the same four teenagers, now more plainly visible, in a warehouse, gathered around a laptop.

Adam (voice-over)

I would set a scenario, and run things from a central location.

Four devices are shown, apparently homemade, some of which appear to use a video-game-controller form factor. They each have screens, keypads, joystick controllers, and SLR-type lenses.

Adam (voice-over)

Each member of the team had a different kind of camera and a specific task to complete. And we were always on a clock. Had to make it seem real.

An image appears of a warehouse, and a title is superimposed on it: ***field test: 14****.*

Adam (voice-over)

This was field test 14, pretty standard for us.

A satellite image appears of a waterside warehouse with boat access.

Adam (voice-over)

We used one of those old marine warehouses, off Harbor Avenue on Puget Sound.

A blueprint is shown next, showing two wet docks side by side.

Adam (voice-over)

Nobody knew we were there. Nobody cared. This time the team had to locate and deactivate markers.

Radiating circles of different colors appear to indicate the locations of markers on the blueprint.

Adam (voice-over)

It had to be about something, right? Had to put the equipment through some paces.

An image of a male African-American teenager appears.

Adam (voice-over)

Here's Finn. He's fearless. And I've never met anyone like him.

The view switches to someone's helmet-cam as he or she locates a quantity of markers laid out on a warehouse floor.

Adam (voice-over)

He's got twenty-four markers to pick up in a very short amount of time. But that's only half of it.

Then the camera switches briefly to a handheld video device directed at Finn.

Finn

Now you *know* I got this, right?

The subject appears to turn on a camera mounted at the rear of a skateboard, and he proceeds to take off at high speed and begin picking up markers. We see him briefly from an overhead security-type camera, and then the image recedes into a set of four images, with the names FINN, EMILY, ADAM, and LEWIS superimposed.

Adam (voice-over)

As usual, all the Trackers were on the move.

The image of the suspect named Lewis fills the screen.

Adam (voice-over)

Every team has to have a Lewis. When everybody else is all hyped up, you need someone who you know is gonna have his feet firmly planted on the ground.

The image is replaced by a warehouse security camera shot showing one of the wet docks. Lewis is walking with a communications device.

Adam (voice-over)

He's got just one marker to find, but it's a little tricky. And he always goes for the shiniest thing first! It's like a joke, and I get him every time.

A label is created over the footage: **ENTER SUPERZOOM MODE**. *A rectangle is superimposed which appears joystick-controlled. It surrounds a shiny spherical object mounted on the warehouse wall.*

Adam (voice-over)

See? There he goes, right on schedule.

The sphere is enlarged and goes through successive sharpening passes until a message, etched in its front surface, becomes clear: **YOU'RE WASTING TIME.** *The image switches back to Lewis, who looks into the lens.*

Lewis

Awkward . . .

The image becomes one of the four in the quadrant, and then Emily's image fills the screen.

Adam (voice-over)

What can I say about Emily? I don't know anyone who has the capacity to focus like she can.

Still images of parts of remote-control vehicles fill the frame in rapid succession.

Adam (voice-over)

She's got this thing for remote-control monster trucks. She's got a wireless cam on this truck, and she uses the Trinity camera as the remote.

Arrows and other symbols illustrate what is being explained. The next images show Emily looking at piles of debris, apparently trying to figure out what she's supposed to do.

Adam (voice-over)

We scattered pieces of a ramp that she can use to launch the truck across the water to where the marker is, but she's gotta figure it out first.

In a security-camera shot, we see that she is walking near one of the wet docks, followed by a remote-control vehicle. The image shrinks into one of the quadrants and the video image with Finn's name on it fills the screen, a helmet-cam sequence showing him climbing narrow stairs to a door with a combination lock on it.

Adam (voice-over)

So Finn entered the eleven-digit code and got himself into the Green Lantern. He knows that code better than his own phone number.

At the top, Finn hesitates briefly, his hand poised over a numeric keypad next to a door; he waggles his fingers in anticipation, then dives into a number sequence. We hear a resounding click as the door unlocks.

Finn

That's what I'm talking about. . . .

We pass through the doorway, and the helmet-cam image shows that Finn is standing at the top of an indoor half-pipe. He identifies a marker on a small shelf at the far side of the half-pipe.

Adam (voice-over)

His last marker is up there on that little platform, right where it's really hard to snag — if you intend to stay on your board.

The perspective appears to switch between several security-cams in the space, Finn's helmet-cam, and a camera mounted on his skateboard. Finn drops in and moves quickly back and forth, apparently trying to get his trajectory and speed correct for an approach to the marker. The image shrinks into one quadrant and the image marked LEWIS *fills the frame.*

Adam (voice-over)

This is where the whole thing started falling apart. I can't say that Lewis failed his part of the mission because he *did* find the marker. Unfortunately, he lost a very expensive piece of equipment.

In a security-camera shot we can see Lewis drop something in the water.

Adam (voice-over)

Finn had a similar outcome.

The image shrinks into one of the quadrants and the video with Finn's name on it fills the screen. Finn is seen skateboarding on a half-pipe. He appears to crash and the video connection is lost. Camera connection is briefly restored and Finn is seen holding the marker.

Finn

I got it!

Adam (voice-over)

He got the marker, but killed the camera.

The image returns to the four quadrants, and the section with Emily's name fills the screen. Emily appears to be in a warehouse. She sets down what appears to be a remote-controlled monster truck and drives it up a ramp. Screen switches to what appears to be a camera on the monster truck.

Adam (voice-over)

Emily and I are still arguing about this one. She's got this theory about updrafts and wind shear. And I've got a theory about hitting the gas too hard and overshooting the target. This was one time when all of Emily's hard work went up in flames. Literally.

Screen enters slo-mo mode. Monster truck appears to explode into a ball of fire. Screen then changes to image of Finn, Adam, Lewis, and Emily sitting around a laptop.

Adam (voice-over)

This mission was pretty huge in terms of equipment loss. But I think of it now as the last time we had a mission where the only thing at stake was busted gadgets.

CLOSE VFILE 2630

APPENDIX B

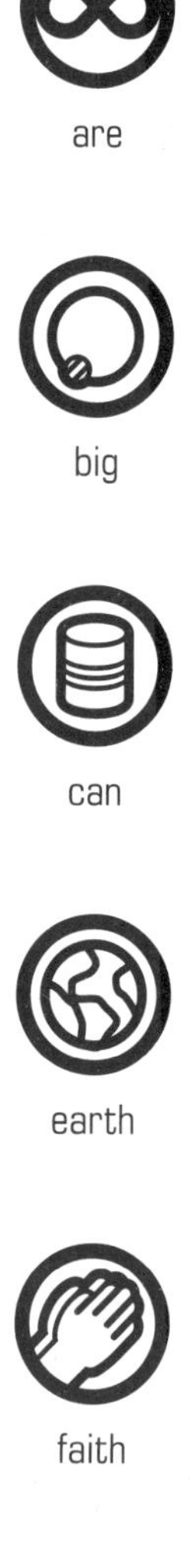

a after all and any

are bad be before beginning

big bike booger boy but

can church day do down

earth eight emergency end even

faith find first five flat

four
girl
give
go
good
government
hard
have
hear
here
how
i
in
just
left
less
level
lock
make
might
moon
more
most
move
much
new
nine
no
not
now
off
old
on
one
out

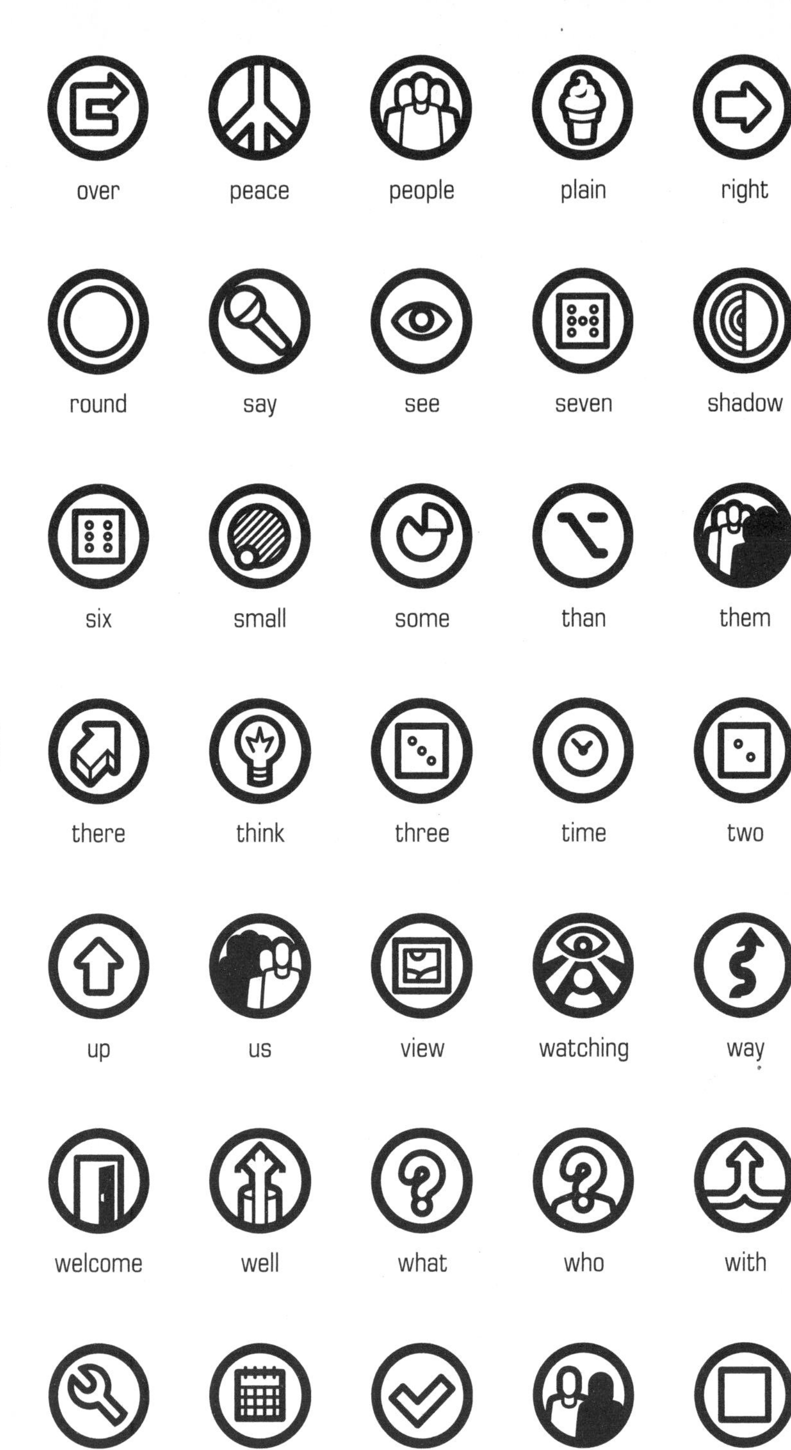
over
peace
people
plain
right
round
say
see
seven
shadow
six
small
some
than
them
there
think
three
time
two
up
us
view
watching
way
welcome
well
what
who
with
work
year
yes
you
zero

APPENDIX C

The following is a transcript of the video shown by Adam Henderson at 18:34 to H. Ganz in Room 214. Transcription and analysis by H. Ganz.

OPEN VFILE 2631

Adam (voice-over)

Here's that security-camera footage from outside the warehouse.

We see an unidentified exterior warehouse door from a security camera. A young woman is seen carrying a folding stool up to the door. She stands on the stool, reaches up, and tucks a small piece of paper next to the door. Image is then greatly enlarged and a close-up is rendered of the young woman wearing sunglasses and partially obscuring her face with her hand.

Adam (voice-over)

I zoomed in to try to get a better look at her face. I know you can't see much, but I was convinced this was the same person who was in this next video.

The image changes to reveal a young woman obscured by shadows and seated in a room in front of a window.

Young Woman

Hi, I'm Zara. Thanks for responding to my challenge. If you're seeing this message, it means you've already solved the first one.

So . . . congratulations. There are only two more levels, but each is a lot more difficult than the one before. Now, don't be too hard on yourself if this is the only level you can complete. It still places you in a rarefied category—trust me. For instance, it means you know something about the symbol language known as Glyph. Some of you will assume that I was involved in that project, the legendary Glyph project, but I wasn't. It's just something I picked up.

If any of you actually make it to the third level—and really, that might not even happen—I can say this: A prize of indescribable value awaits the winner. I won't say any more than that. Keep an eye on the puzzle site. You'll know when it's time to continue. And time is definitely a factor here. Good luck.

The image freezes, then zooms in.

Adam (voice-over)

Turns out, I was going to need a lot more than luck.

CLOSE VFILE 2631

APPENDIX D

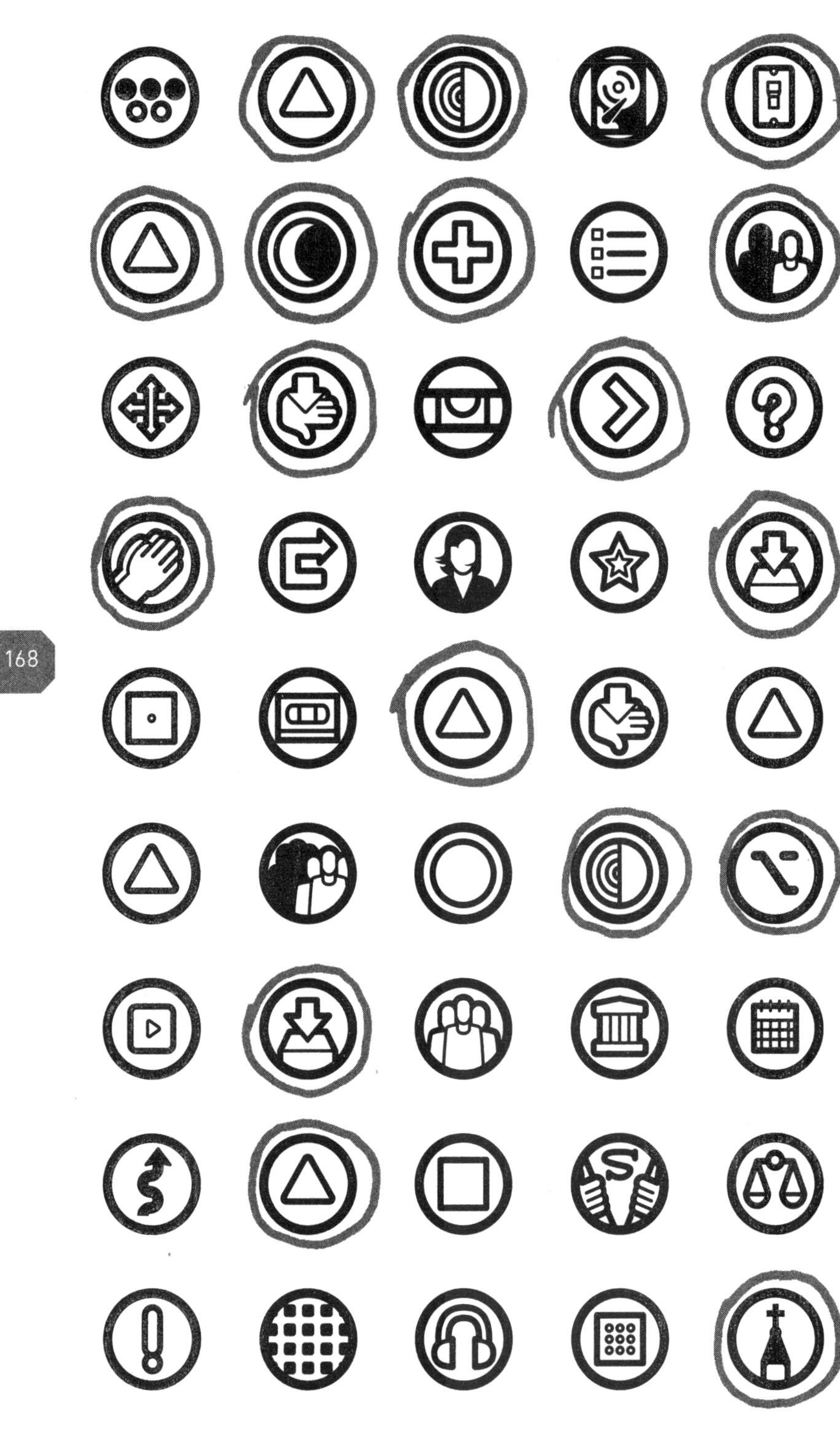

APPENDIX E

The following is a transcript of the video shown by Adam Henderson at 19:00 to H. Ganz in Room 214. Transcription and analysis by H. Ganz.

OPEN VFILE 2632

It's Zara again, same room, same window. Another light has been turned on, making her somewhat easier to identify.

Zara

Hello, Adam. Yes, this message is just for you. Nicely done. That second level has seriously thinned out the crowd. I saw how you approached the solve, and I was impressed. Very nice work.

She hesitates here.

Zara

In fact . . . I think we should meet. Let's do this: If you can finish the puzzle, I will go to that coffee shop near you—what's it called? The Grind House?—I'll be there at two P.M., the day you reach the final level. Excuse me—*if* you reach the final level. But you're good. Maybe a little too good . . . We'll just have to see.

The image freezes and zooms in slowly.

Adam (voice-over)

Well, I knew the game had changed, but there was so much I still didn't know.

CLOSE VFILE 2632

APPENDIX F

The following is a transcript of the video shown by Adam Henderson at 19:36 to H. Ganz in Room 214. Transcription and analysis by H. Ganz.

OPEN VFILE 2633

From a ceiling-mounted security camera, we see a man entering the computer repair store. The shop's owner (later identified as the suspect's father) is seen handing an unidentified item, possibly a hard drive, to the man.

Adam (voice-over)

There was hours of footage to go through, but I found the part where the guy came in.

Customer

Hi.

Adam (voice-over)

This is my dad, by the way.

Before leaving, the customer turns around and tips his hat directly to the security camera.

Adam (voice-over)

All right. Check this out.

The video rewinds and zooms in to show a grainy image of the customer looking directly at the security camera.

Adam (voice-over)

So here he is. Say hello to my own personal nightmare.

The image changes to a close-up of a man, mid-forties, speaking with an Eastern European accent, addressing the camera in an unknown setting. He bears more than a passing resemblance to the customer in the previous video.

Adam (voice-over)

And this is that file I found hidden on one of my drives.

Man

Let me start by making a guess. You are thinking, right about now, that you should be calling the police. Am I right?

Adam (voice-over)

He had me there. That's exactly what I was thinking.

Man

And, uh, you will tell 'em what? Someone copied files off of your hard drive? What is the value of these files? Don't you still have your own copies? "But my files are valuable to me."

Adam (voice-over)

Let's just get this straight. I do not talk like that, okay?

Man

Be glad that you still have them. Go home. Play a video game.

Adam (voice-over)

All right. This is where he laid it all out.

Man

You and I know perfectly well what has happened here. You have, quite possibly, one of the most magnificent portfolios of cutting-edge inventions from, from, Helsinki to Tokyo.

Adam (voice-over)

Okay. Now, that's something every decent programmer wants to hear.

Man

I want you to do exactly what I say. If you are a man of your word, if you can be trusted to do as I ask, I will destroy my copy of that magnificent portfolio of inventions. But I'm being rude. A friend of yours would like to say hello.

Adam (voice-over)

I'd like to say I saw this coming, but I didn't.

The man picks up a small remote control, aims it at the camera, and the camera pans over to reveal the young woman, known as Zara, from the previous two files.

Zara

Hello, Adam. I'm glad it was you who solved the puzzle. You were always my favorite.

She smiles and the image goes black.

CLOSE VFILE 2633

» APPENDIX G

The following is a transcript of the video shown by Adam Henderson at 20:42 to H. Ganz in Room 214. Transcription and analysis by H. Ganz.

OPEN VFILE 2634 A

A security camera shows us a high view of an establishment that has been confirmed as the Grind House.

Adam (voice-over)

So here we had the same event covered from three very different perspectives. Finn was inside by the entrance. Emily was outside a few doors down. And I was in the balcony, waiting for Zara and trying not to fall asleep. This first video shows the feed from Finn's camera, the Belinski, and a pirated signal we picked up from a security camera at the Grind House. Finn knows that where there's coffee, there's sugar, so that's where he's headed.

Image shows Finn moving away from the mobile camera he has set up near entrance, over to where the café places cream and sugar for customers' use.

Emily (offscreen)

Lazlo's on the move! Guys!

As Finn appears to ingest a packet of sugar, the suspect identified as Lazlo appears in the foreground.

Adam (voice-over)

And Lazlo must have had some way of seeing, because that's the exact moment he appears . . .

Lazlo leans close to the camera.

Lazlo

(whispering)

Stop watching us.

Adam (voice-over)

. . . and makes off with the Belinski.

Lazlo exits the Grind House with the video device called the Belinski in his right hand, then appears to drop it into a garbage can. The camera appears to fail shortly after impact.

CLOSE VFILE 2634 A

OPEN VFILE 2634 B

Emily is seen peering out from a recessed doorway, looking up and down an unidentified street. She sees something, and the image switches to a different view from the same camera device to see Lazlo approaching the Grind House. The image switches back to Emily.

Adam (voice-over)

Emily was outside and caught Lazlo's arrival.

Emily

Lazlo's on the move! Guys!

Adam (voice-over)

And swift departure.

This is apparently the same moment that we've just seen, photographed from Emily's position outside. She switches back to the main camera just in time to see Lazlo leave with a leather portfolio in his left hand. His right hand is not visible. She retreats deeper into the recessed doorway, which obscures our view for a moment. When she pulls the camera back up, we can see Lazlo moving away, toward the corner of the block. She takes off after him. He makes a turn and she moves to a vantage point near the corner. Zara is in a black late-model SUV on the passenger side.

Adam (voice-over)

Turns out, Zara was right around the corner when I was talking to her.

Zara rolls down her window, and Lazlo hands her the portfolio, crossing behind the car to get in on the driver's side. He starts the car and they drive off. Camera view changes to show Emily.

Emily

I think I got something just then.

Adam (voice-over)

And Emily was right. She did get something just then. Something huge. But we couldn't see it—not yet anyway.

CLOSE VFILE 2634 B

OPEN VFILE 2634 C

A view of Adam from his own Webcam, seated in what appears to be the loft area of the Grind House. Suspect appears fatigued. A voice from his own device is heard.

Zara (offscreen)

I told you I'd be here.

Adam stares at the device in front of him. We switch to an apparently fabricated image of his device on the table with Zara's image visible on its screen.

Adam (voice-over)

I made this to show how weird it was to have Zara just appear like that on the prototype I'd brought.

Zara

It's reassuring that you actually showed up. Not so happy about all the friends you brought along.

Adam

How are you doing this?

Zara

I'm going to ask you not to move from the balcony

there, if that's all right with you. It's what Lazlo wants, and trust me, you don't want to cross him.

We see text superimposed on Adam's screen:

GPS ACTIVATED

Adam

Just keep him away from my friends.

Adam (voice-over)

I was trying to keep an eye on things, but she did her job. She totally distracted me from what Lazlo was doing.

Adam appears to be trying to locate Finn and looks concerned.

Zara

You asked me how I'm doing this.

Adam

Right.

Zara

Seems like you left something in the water. Kudos to you for designing the watertight seal for the case.

Adam

How did you get it?

Zara

Really, Adam, you should always have at least *one* person on your team who scuba dives.

Adam

And I bet you scuba dive.

Zara

For years. The real question is, how far are you willing to go to get your inventions back?

Adam

Well, what are we talking about here?

Zara appears to be looking at something else, perhaps another device, for just a moment.

Zara

Sorry, I think you'll be hearing from Emily in just a second. . . .

Emily (offscreen)

Lazlo's on the move! Guys!

Adam appears to be scanning the crowd in the café for Lazlo.

Zara

Okay, well, maybe we could have coffee for real sometime. . . .

Zara terminates her connection.

Adam (voice-over)

I was really tired, but I still shouldn't have let it happen.

CLOSE VFILE 2634 C

APPENDIX H

The following is a transcript of the video shown by Adam Henderson at 22:15 to H. Ganz in Room 214. Transcription and analysis by H. Ganz.

OPEN VFILE 2635

Lewis is standing in an unidentified exterior location.

Adam (voice-over)

Lewis was involved in developing the Deckard's feature set, and it shows. He put that thing through its paces — with awesome results.

Lewis

Okay. This is what I've been working on. I took the footage of Zara from the game. I was looking for anything that could help us locate her.

Image switches to a still of Zara as seen in a previous video.

Lewis

So I spent way too much time trying to identify the curtains, the furniture, and the little statue on the windowsill behind her. And then it struck me: I'm looking at the wrong thing. So I thought, what if I darken it and see if there's any detail hiding in the sky outside?

The image darkens to reveal a church steeple in the distance. The image zooms in to show a closer view.

Lewis

So, hello, we've got some information now. Information they didn't know they were giving us.

The view of Lewis outside returns.

Lewis

You're not going to believe it—I found that church! I'm a few blocks away, but I got a good vantage point, so I shot some photos.

View changes to a photograph of the church steeple. Lewis appears to be applying 3-D coordinates to the image.

Lewis

So we apply some 3–D coordinates. And then I compare it to the image from her video. We do a little GPS extrapolation . . .

The image changes to a GPS satellite map.

Lewis

Figure out which side this is, and we see it's the south side. Now all we have to do is calculate an approximate distance. The only building tall enough to get that perspective is going to be . . .

We see Lewis reading off the screen on his device.

Lewis

. . . the Windsor Residential Hotel.

Adam (voice-over)

So now we knew that Lazlo's and Zara's videos were made over at the Windsor. I had a few ideas on figuring out which room they were in.

Emily appears on the screen in what appears to be a residential setting.

Adam (voice-over)

Emily sent this in later. Man, she really knows how to get the most out of the Trinity.

Emily types on her computer.

Emily

Okay, buddy, show us what you got there. . . .

The image switches to the shot of Lazlo passing the portfolio to Zara in the car. Text appears onscreen: ***ENTER SLO-MO MODE****. The playback begins at normal speed and then enters a very high frame-rate playback mode. A cyclist briefly obscures our view of the movements of the portfolio between the two suspects. Text appears onscreen:* ***ENLARGE AND ENHANCE****. A segment of the image from the front of the portfolio is enlarged and sharpened, and eventually we can see the gold-stamped name on the front of the portfolio:* ***BLACKFOOT HOLDINGS****.*

Emily

Blackfoot Holdings? I guess it's kind of obvious, but we have to try, right?

We see suspect Emily enter blackfootholdings.com into her Web browser. The image changes to a Web page for Blackfoot Holdings. A video plays on the Web site. A male voice, a possible match for Lazlo, speaks over quiet music.

Man's Voice

Blackfoot Holdings, an international investment company specializing in wealth management for individuals and corporations of distinction. Isn't it time you joined our team?

We see Emily again.

Emily

Weird, huh? Let's file that under "needs more research." Emily out.

Adam (voice-over)

After some serious digging, it became clear to Emily that Blackfoot Holdings was just some money-laundering scheme, plain and simple.

The image holds on the silhouetted figure seen in the Blackfoot Holdings video, but suspect Adam appears to have superimposed the face of Lazlo over it.

CLOSE VFILE 2635

APPENDIX I

The following is a transcript of the video shown by Adam Henderson at 23:10 to H. Ganz in Room 214. Transcription and analysis by H. Ganz.

OPEN VFILE 2636

Video opens on the satellite map seen in Lewis's prior message, with a yellow box and text identifying the Windsor Hotel.

Adam (voice-over)

First we had to figure out which room they were using. I'd been waiting for the perfect test for the Orville. And this was it.

Suspect is visible, talking into his phone's Webcam, at what appears to be the rear of the Windsor Residential Hotel. He holds up some kind of modified micro-helicopter.

Adam

It's Orville Time.

He releases the device into the air, and the image switches to what appears to be footage transmitted from a camera on the front of the micro-helicopter. The camera begins to scan the windows of the hotel.

Adam (offscreen)

We're looking for a window, maybe on the fifth floor,

maybe on the fourth, with a little statue in the windowsill. . . . I don't know, this seems kind of like a long shot. Oh, wait . . .

The helicopter's camera hovers outside the window of a room with a small decorative statue on its windowsill. Statue appears similar to the one visible in the background of videos of Zara.

Adam (offscreen)

Got it! Looks like the—

(counting)

—fifth window from the elevators, fourth floor up.

An image of suspect Finn appears, exiting an elevator on one of the upper floors of the Windsor Hotel.

Adam (voice-over)

Next, we had to get Finn to figure out which room numbers went with which windows.

Finn appears confused.

Adam (voice-over)

In retrospect, he might have been the wrong guy for the job.

Adam (offscreen)

The elevator opens south. Turn right, look left. . . .

Suspect orients himself and starts reading room numbers. Image switches to suspect Lewis, standing outside.

Finn (offscreen)

It's gotta be either 406 or 408. Let's say from 404 to 410.

Lewis

404 to 410. That's four different keys. . . .

Adam (offscreen)

Is that okay? Can you make four?

Lewis

Yeah, I should be able to. . . .

We cut to a moving shot in the lobby of the hotel.

Adam (voice-over)

Then we had to get the girl at the front desk out of the lobby so Lewis could get some blank keys. There was no talking Finn out of that job. He was seriously not going to let anyone else do it.

The camera, apparently concealed in the shoulder strap of suspect Finn's backpack, shows an unidentified female hotel desk clerk in her twenties.

Finn (offscreen)

Could I get a little help over here?

Desk Clerk

I'll meet you right around this corner.

Finn and the desk clerk are now seen outside the Windsor Hotel. As the clerk points to the south, Finn appears to turn and direct his concealed camera to the north, and Lewis can be seen hurrying into the hotel entrance, unseen.

Adam (voice-over)

Finn got her looking down the street so Lewis could get in without being seen.

The image switches to a device carried by Lewis as he approaches the hotel front desk, reaches over the counter, and grabs four blank key cards.

Adam (voice-over)

I'm still amazed what Lewis could put together with some ribbon cable, a three-dollar processor, a broken card swipe, and an empty breath mint container.

Lewis has pulled out some kind of makeshift hardware and appears to program the stolen hotel key cards.

Adam (voice-over)

Lewis only had time to make three keys before Finn made it around to the employees' entrance. I sent Lewis to let him in.

We see Lewis opening a locked door at the rear of the hotel, allowing Finn to enter. The image switches to Lewis and Finn emerging from the elevator and approaching the first door they have a key card for. Finn knocks. When there is no response, Lewis swipes the card, the door unlocks, and they peer in.

Adam (voice-over)

They started trying the keys.

Lewis (offscreen)

One down.

They move to the next door, and Finn knocks. No one answers. They open the door and take a look, apparently unsatisfied.

Adam (voice-over)

They all worked, thanks to Lewis, but it was looking like maybe we had the wrong room numbers after all.

Lewis (offscreen)

One more card.

Lewis knocks on the third door. When there's no answer, they swipe the card and open the door.

Adam (voice-over)

Then they opened the third room.

Lewis and Finn are seen entering a hotel suite.

Finn

This is it.

Adam (offscreen)

Are you sure?

Lewis switches to a different camera, apparently on the front of his device.

Lewis (offscreen)

See for yourself.

He zooms in on the statue on the windowsill, then pans over the area previously visible in suspect Zara's videos.

Adam (offscreen)

Nice job, guys. Okay, now find a spot for the camera and get out.

Finn takes something out of his device and appears to place it on or near the statue on the windowsill. The image switches to a perspective from that vantage point.

Adam (voice-over)

For some reason, our channels got messed up and they couldn't hear me, which was unfortunate because I was trying to tell them they were about to have visitors.

In the background, Lewis appears to be listening for something.

Lewis

You hear something?

Finn

Hear what?

Lewis

Shh . . .

They both listen in absolute silence. Lewis suddenly looks at the Deckard.

Lewis

Oh, man, I had this on vibrate. . . .

His camera's speaker turns back on and Adam's voice can be heard.

Adam (offscreen)

—under the bed! Now! They're coming!

Lewis and Finn dive under the bed.

Adam (voice-over)

Finn and Lewis told me later it was so cramped under there, they were convinced they were being punked. If only that were the case.

Finn and Lewis are seen under the bed in an infrared or night-vision feed from a camera identified onscreen as the Deckard. Zara and Lazlo are seen entering. Lazlo hands Zara a small device, and as she takes it she hesitates, smiling.

Adam (voice-over)

Here's where Zara got the Raymond device from Lazlo in the nifty case I made for it.

Zara

(to herself)

Nice.

She sits at the computer, inserts the device, and goes to work. Lazlo paces briefly and then hovers over her at the desk.

Adam (voice-over)

Check this out.

Zara

This is all we need to do now. Any evidence that the Raymond back door was opened will be found on Adam's computer, not ours.

Adam (voice-over)

See, she said it. They framed us.

The hotel phone rings. Zara and Lazlo glance at the phone and then look at each other.

Adam (voice-over)

That's me the first time I called, but they didn't pick up. When I called back, I told Zara to put me on speakerphone.

Zara turns on the speakerphone.

Zara

Adam?

Intermittently, Adam's side of the phone call, most likely from the workshop at the rear of his father's store, is seen.

Adam

I want to meet, but not up there, not in the room.

Zara

What did you have in mind?

Adam

The lobby. Meet me there. That's where I am.

Lazlo

Adam, this is Lazlo.

Adam

I know.

Lazlo

It'll be best if we stay right here.

Adam

Really? What if I told you I can see everything Zara's doing; you're only one step away from the back door.

Zara

And all I have to do is hit ENTER.

Adam

Do you fully understand what you're doing?

Lazlo

What about you, Adam? Are you sure you fully understand?

Adam

We know all about Blackfoot Holdings. We know it's how you plan to launder the money.

Lazlo and Zara exchange a glance and she touches a key on the laptop. The image switches to what appears to be a pirated signal from her screen: A puzzle previously identified as The Glyphmaster appears. Zara looks at Lazlo.

Zara

I told you.

Adam

What's going on?

Lazlo

(to Zara)

Yes, you did.

Adam (voice-over)

What was up with that response? Totally not what I was expecting.

Lazlo turns and sits on the bed. The night-vision image of Lewis and Finn underneath him, reacting, appears briefly.

Lazlo

You can come out from under the bed now.

Adam

I'm not under the bed.

Lazlo

I wasn't talking to you, Adam. I was talking to Finn and Lewis.

Adam

Guys! Run for it!

Lazlo

Nice and slow, please.

Finn and Lewis emerge from under the bed.

Zara

Can we just get Adam and Emily here now so we can talk this through?

Adam

I think I'm ready to get the police involved. . . .

Lazlo

I don't think that's a good idea. I'm not threatening your friends. Bring Emily. We will explain everything.

Adam (voice-over)

I didn't want to go. I wanted to call the cops. I kept thinking, it's safer if I'm here where I can see everything.

Adam's image flickers and freezes.

Adam (voice-over)

But I had no choice. Lewis and Finn were in real trouble this time and I'd put them there. I had to go.

Adam is seen running out of the repair shop.

Zara (offscreen)

Adam? Adam?

CLOSE VFILE 2636

APPENDIX J

The following is a transcript of the video shown by Adam Henderson at 23:35 to H. Ganz in Room 214. Transcription and analysis by H. Ganz.

OPEN VFILE 2637

Suspect Adam, apparently carrying his phone with its Webcam turned on, and suspect Emily approach a hotel room door and knock.

Adam (voice-over)

Emily and I went up to the room. I had the Orville running in case I needed the evidence later.

Lazlo opens the door and waves them in.

Lazlo

Come in. Make yourselves comfortable.

Adam (voice-over)

I was relieved to see that Lewis had turned on the Deckard and was secretly filming, too. It was eerie, walking into that room, everybody just standing there.

Suspect Lazlo reaches into a jacket pocket and offers Adam what appears to be a business card. Finn finds a chair and sits down.

Lazlo

We are with ISD, the Internet Security Directive . . .

A close-up of the card Lazlo handed Adam appears onscreen.

INTERNET SECURITY DIRECTIVE

888-555-0001 (MEMORIZE AND DESTROY)

Adam (voice-over)

I guess I wasn't supposed to keep the card. Woops!

Lazlo

. . . a highly classified federal agency. We recruit all the best programmers and technicians . . .

Adam (voice-over)

He explained that ISD hires programmer types to go after hackers who are into cyber theft on a pretty big scale.

Lazlo

. . . defraud and steal via the Internet.

Finn

No way . . .

Adam

You guys are Feds?

Zara

It's how we had to play it.

Emily

Wait, why should we believe you now?

Lewis

Yeah, anyone can make a business card. . . .

Lazlo

Well, your hesitation is understandable. The puzzles, the clues that led you to us—all of it was just an elaborate test devised only for you.

Adam

Wait, when you say everything . . .

Zara

Yeah. The Glyphmaster site? Blackfoot Holdings?

A screen capture of each Web site is shown here.

Zara

Those were IP address–specific sites. Only you could see them. The rest of the world sees a page that says "server not found."

A screen capture of the error-message page appears.

Adam (voice-over)

I never thought of making Web sites that only certain people could find.

Lazlo

All the cases that we've closed so far are child's play compared to the one we have before us right now. This is the one which we cannot fail.

Adam

The Raymond back door?

Zara

The Raymond device we have is real, you know that now, but what you don't know is that it's not the only one.

Lazlo

The other one is in the hands of someone who used to work for us. A remarkable programmer. When he disappeared, we realized right away we had made a mistake, but it was too late.

Adam (voice-over)

I think we all started to sense what was coming.

Zara

He's a legend in the world of hackers—we should have seen it.

Adam (voice-over)

And who they were describing.

Emily

Are we talking about Shantorian?

Lazlo nods.

Adam

That guy used to work for you?

Finn

I remember you talking about that guy. . . .

Lewis

He's the hacker of all hackers! This guy can do anything!

Lazlo

Where he is now, nobody knows for sure.

Zara

The Raymond back door is a huge threat. And we're hearing about a new Shantorian virus. Things like this are dangerous on a scale that can only be described as massive. The world's economies are at risk.

Lazlo

We are still recruiting operatives so we can close the Raymond back door for good.

Zara

And put Shantorian behind bars.

Finn

I'm not a programmer.

Emily

Neither am I.

Zara

But you're Trackers.

No one speaks.

Lazlo

ISD needs Adam's inventions. We need trackers.

Adam (voice-over)

Lazlo had tricked us before, but this was different. It was a chance to do something that really mattered.

Lazlo

So. Are you guys ready for your last test?

An awkward moment of silence. Everyone appears to be trying to assess the others' reactions.

Adam (voice-over)

I knew what he was capable of. The test would be dangerous. Someone might even get hurt.

CLOSE VFILE 2637

APPENDIX K

The following is a transcript of the video shown by Adam Henderson at 23:51 to H. Ganz in Room 214. Transcription and analysis by H. Ganz.

OPEN VFILE 2638

Screen opens with a several views of a large decommissioned power station (provisionally identified as PGE 133).

Adam (voice-over)

Lazlo and Zara gave us the address of an old power station south of town. In some ways, it was like our own field test. In other ways, it was a whole new ball game. The only instructions we had were to come equipped, whatever that meant, and to pay close attention to the red lines. I made sure Finn had a full set of Minicams charged up. Emily packed some stuff that I'd never seen before. Lewis suggested he take the Orville's chopper and a few other things with him. Each Tracker had a different start point in the building.

Lewis is seen from a camera that appears to be mounted on or near the handlebars of a bike. He walks the bike toward a large doorway, apparently inside the power station.

Adam (voice-over)

Lewis was up first. When he saw what his mission was, he knew they must have been watching him closely.

Lewis

Okay, I'm, uh—wait . . . Yeah, I'm ready!

Image appears to switch to his helmet-cam and can now see into a space nearly three stories tall. A homemade stunt course has been set up, about four feet off the floor, fabricated from broken pallets and other scraps of wood.

Adam (voice-over)

It was the sketchiest stunt course any of us had ever seen.

Zara's voice can be heard from time to time in this video, apparently broadcast on some kind of PA system.

Zara (offscreen)

Don't forget about the red line. . . .

Lewis

I don't think I really could, Zara.

Lewis pushes off and follows a red line on the floor that leads to a narrow ramp. He rides up the ramp and follows the twists and turns of the course, picking up speed as he goes. There are at least four security-camera views included here, as well as the handlebar-cam and the helmet-cam already seen. The course ends abruptly, four feet off the ground. Lewis takes the jump on his bike and follows another red line to a nearby area with two dozen small orange cones.

Adam (voice-over)

When he landed, he saw what looked like a really basic dexterity course with cones. That didn't seem right.

And so he pulled out the Deckard and started looking more closely at the cones.

Lewis pulls a device out of his backpack and aims its lens at the cone area. Four of the cones are singled out with circular indicators on a freeze frame taken by the camera.

Adam (voice-over)

There were tiny numbers on four of them.

Text is superimposed on the image: ***ENTER SUPERZOOM MODE****. Portions of the image that include the tops of the four highlighted cones are enlarged somewhere between 600 and 1,000 percent. Handwritten numerals are visible in the enlarged images:* ***2****,* ***5****,* ***3****, and* ***9****.*

Adam (voice-over)

We didn't know what they meant, but it seemed like we were supposed to find them.

Lewis (offscreen)

Are you getting this, Adam?

Adam (offscreen)

Two five three nine—I'll start working on that. Emily, you there?

Adam (voice-over)

Then it was Emily's turn.

The image switches to Emily's Webcam.

Emily

Ready to roll!

Adam (voice-over)

She said later on it was like someone had been taking notes during her nightmares. She's tough, but she just doesn't like creepy and spooky places.

She appears to carry her device at arm's length as she descends a narrow staircase into the basement of the power station. There is less and less light as she proceeds.

Emily (offscreen)

(muttering to herself)

Red line, red line . . .

Emily appears to stumble over something.

Adam (voice-over)

She had to put the Trinity in night-vision mode just to see where she was going. She found a door, but then she saw something I don't think anyone else would have noticed . . .

In infrared or night-vision mode, a door is visible. The camera is directed up and to the right. A device like a small flashlight is mounted at the corner of the doorjamb. Suspect produces a small spray bottle and uses its mist to illuminate a red laser beam, crossing the doorway at an angle.

Adam (voice-over)

. . . and she used a silicone-based spray to confirm it. A laser was aimed across the doorway as a kind of trip wire. It was the red line she was looking for.

She pulls something else out of her backpack: a cylindrical object measuring about an inch by half an inch. She attaches the device directly in front of the beam's source, blocking the laser's path.

Adam (voice-over)

She used a tiny, front-surface mirror to trick the laser into thinking it was still beaming across the door.

Emily opens the door. An office with simple, older furnishings is visible.

Adam (voice-over)

Once she got inside, she did a quick search of what seemed to be somebody's old office, but nothing really stood out. Then she realized . . .

On top of the filing cabinet, a cageless fan is operating.

Emily (offscreen)

Okay, well, who leaves a fan running in an abandoned office?

Adam (voice-over)

When she saw there was no Off switch, she decided to use the Trinity to check out her hunch.

The camera is aimed directly at the rotating blades of the fan. Text is superimposed: **ENTER SLO-MO MODE**. *The turning of the blades slows abruptly.*

Emily (offscreen)

Okay, wait. Let me see. Get there . . .

Four numbers, etched by hand into one of the blades, are now visible. The image freezes: ***8366***.

Adam (voice-over)

And there it was . . .

Emily (offscreen)

Got that?

Adam (voice-over)

. . . another four-digit number. And I still had no idea what to do with it.

The image switches to a wireless feed with heavy interference, showing a dozen or so concrete steps. Image is consistent with helmet-cam or similar footage.

Adam (voice-over)

Finn's mission started out bad and got worse from there. He started to lose his signal.

A voice consistent with Finn's can be heard here, but the signal is interrupted by heavy interference.

Adam (voice-over)

But to make matters worse, he was supposed to make this insane stair jump.

Adam (offscreen)

Finn, there's something wrong with your signal. I'm going to try to find another channel for you to use.

We see a length of red twine suspended over the concrete stairs. A sound like a skateboard can be heard over the interference, and a brief movement, suggesting a stair jump was executed by Finn, is visible here. Audio suggests a hard landing. After some transmission noise, hands and feet consistent with Finn are seen standing up and dusting off. Helmet-cam footage is indicated here.

Adam (voice-over)

Finn's board fell into a lower platform after the jump. He noticed there was a red line pointing at the door down there. He was about to step onto the platform to check it out when he decided to stick a Minicam on the railing to give me another view.

Finn is visible placing a wireless cam, and the image shows that he has picked up his skateboard and is on a ladder.

Adam (voice-over)

Good thing he did. Those Minicams weigh—I don't know—maybe an ounce and a half? But I guess it was an ounce and a half too many.

The platform that the wireless cam is on appears to pull away from the wall and topple over backward. A very loud crash can be heard, consistent with a large structure collapsing. Image becomes unstable and goes black.

Adam (voice-over)

The whole platform gave out.

Finn's helmet-cam appears to show that he safely returns to the upper platform.

Adam (voice-over)

He got back up to safety, but there was no way to get through that door now. I was stumped. But the next thing I know, he's hopping up and down like a jackrabbit.

From Finn's helmet-cam, an empty ceramic power conduit can be seen, ten feet or so up on a brick wall.

Adam (voice-over)

He was trying to tell me he found a hole in the wall big enough for the Orville's chopper. Lewis pulled it out of his backpack and I controlled it from here.

An image consistent with the remote helicopter seen before flies toward and then through the funnel in the wall and into a large, open space elsewhere in the power station.

Adam (voice-over)

The room was pretty big and there were a lot of places to hide a four-digit number—if that's even what we were supposed to find. I kept thinking, how small could they be? Or how big? And I pulled way up in the corner and tilted the chopper down toward the floor.

*From a high vantage point, it appears someone has used a broom or mop to push the dust on the floor into the shape of four numbers: **3746**.*

Adam (voice-over)

Sure enough, a gigantic four-digit number. Nothing like a little perspective to show you something new.

The image changes to show a classic telephone dial pad, with three or four letters beneath each numeral.

Adam (voice-over)

Lewis suggested using a phone keypad layout to try turning the numbers into letters. I ran it through an app that usually does a good job at showing you the most likely letter combinations. Still looked totally random.

We see the following groups of letters on the screen:

CLEW
TEMO
DSIO

Adam (voice-over)

Then Emily said to reverse the order of each group of four letters.

The groups of letters are rearranged as described:

WELC
OMET
OISD

Adam (voice-over)

And right when I did that, a video window popped up on everyone's screens.

The screen changes and a box with a video image of Lazlo appears.

Lazlo

Good job, team.

A second box appears alongside the first one, with Zara's image in it.

Lazlo

Very nice work.

Zara

Yes, and that message was for all of you.

Adam (offscreen)

Which message?

Zara

This message.

The stacked letters are rearranged on one line and two spaces inserted.

WELCOME TO ISD

Zara (offscreen)

Welcome to ISD.

The four suspects are seen congratulating each other.

Adam (voice-over)

I can still remember how pumped we were. We'd made it. We were working for ISD.

Over black, a heartbeat can be heard. Two images of Lazlo appear and fade out.

Adam (voice-over)

But there would always be a part of me that wondered whether we could trust Lazlo.

Two images of Zara appear and fade out.

Adam (voice-over)

And in a lot of ways, Zara was even more of a mystery than before.

The screen goes black. The heartbeat sound continues.

Adam (voice-over)

We were in. That was a good thing. But the question remained: What had we actually gotten ourselves into?

CLOSE VFILE 2638

TRACKERS CREDITS

CAST

Adam	James Murray
Zara	Morgan Hopper
Finn	Urijah Sailes
Emily	Chloe Danielson
Lewis	John Shaw
Lazlo	Eric Derovanessian

CREW

Director	Jeffrey Townsend
Writer / Producer	Patrick Carman
Associate Producer	Alex English
Director of Photography	Brandon Lehman
Art Director	Jason Daub
Video Editors	Jason Daub
	Jeffrey Townsend
Assistant Director	Chris Cresci
Book Editor	David Levithan
Assistant Editor	Gregory Rutty
Production Editor	Joy Simpkins
Book Design	Christopher Stengel
Designer / Web Developer	Joshua Pease
3-D Models	Straightface Studios / Don Lange
Prop Design	Luke Chilson
Prop Fabrication	Victor Trejo
Hair / Makeup Consultant	Amy Vories

Hair / Makeup / Wardrobe Supervisor	Darcy Sturges
Hair / Makeup / Wardrobe Assistant	Shane Wood
Production Consultants	Sarah Koenigsberg
	Amber Larsen
Casting Associates	Lindsey Daub
	Jennifer Elkington
	Tiffany Talent, Tanya Tiffany
	Cari Wilton
Production Assistants	Amanda Hamilton
	Anna Hinz
	Elizabeth Shaw
Chaperones / Transportation	Jimmy Murray
	Theresa Sailes
Hospitality	Karen Carman
	Patrice Townsend

Vehicles	Ford of Walla Walla / Kirk Williams
Catering	Graze / John Lastoskie
Insurance	State Farm / Liz Conover

SPECIAL THANKS

Alan Ketelson and Sonia Schmitt
Banner Bank (Doug Bayne)
Davis Shows (Pat, Geraldine, and Manny Davis)
Exemplar Real Estate (Barb Whatley)
Marcus Whitman Hotel (Shanna Hatfield and Kris Garten)
Mason Helms and Kenneth Butler
Merchants Ltd. (Bob Austin)
Port of Walla Walla (Paul Gerola)
Walla Walla Police Department
Walla Walla University (Jerry Hartman)